The Laughter of Sanity

The Laughter of Sanity

Richard Amiss

RESOURCE *Publications* · Eugene, Oregon

THE LAUGHTER OF SANITY

Resource Publications
An Imprint of Wipf and Stock Publishers
199 W. 8th Ave., Suite 3
Eugene, OR 97401

www.wipfandstock.com

PAPERBACK ISBN: 978-1-7252-7295-8
HARDCOVER ISBN: 978-1-7252-7294-1
EBOOK ISBN: 978-1-7252-7296-5

04/28/21

Dedicated to The Immaculate Conception

For Beth
Thank you Lord!

Contents

Chapter One: **Behind Blue Eyes**

T he subtle breeze and the invisible energy that drove the wind caused the old man to pause. Eli stretched out his back and stood up straight. He thought of the day he would see his daughter again and he knew the moment she would arrive. Eager for that day, a private revelation surfaced in his heart. Eli's fondness for her surpassed immeasurable. Many people would come to know her. Because of the love she expressed for others, she attracted them. His son died and he didn't talk about his death. The sun pressed down on him as he leaned over to snap off dead flowers in the garden he attended to. During his career as a gardener, he enjoyed the still-ness of all the plants and the silence within. The state park gave him the job because of how much he knew about trees and plant life.

He looked to be around seventy to eighty years old and he moved like a whale in the ocean. Eyes, a deep blue and clear. He appeared very old and yet young. The modern world was fast and many admired his pace. When he spoke to those passing by, his words came out as if each took a firm step on the ground.

The gardens, a place of peace not be thought. Once in a while, people would comment on his work with admiration and he showed complete humility. All the plants and flowers that he attended to and took care of displayed a stillness like him on the inside. His invisible essence that he carried contained light, which people paid attention to more than his physical form.

Eli and his daughter would meet at different places around the world as they traveled and spent time together. She visited many places and ex-perienced being welcomed, no matter where she went. Neither became bogged down and life and experiences passed through them like the reflec-tions of birds flying over the water.

The garden he took care of bordered right next to the beach. The salty air and humidity married and remained inseparable. A breeze stirred be it at night or day and no matter what time of year. The tips of winter's fingers would rarely reach south Florida. "What winter?" people would often respond. The sound of seagulls repeated crescendos of life as did the surf. People stepped over the hot sand some days like they did a fire walk.

Eli tended to some orchids underneath a towering bougainvillea. The botanical gardens where he worked mirrored a tropical urban oasis featuring an unparalleled horticultural display next to the bay. He spent his career working here, a place more home to him than his little cottage near the beach. It reflected a literal botanist's dream. Next time he and his daughter met, it would be in front of the waterfall, her favorite place. Sometimes, when he wasn't tending to the orchids and bromeliads, he liked to walk along the beach and enjoy life, people and listen to the sound of the surf. The sea breeze mixed with salty humidity. Just walking on the beach barefoot and watching the ocean, the greatest thing in the world, he thought. So much peace, tranquility, and sublime power. The best of both environments surrounded by all the plant life in the botanical gardens and the beautiful coastline of South Florida.

Not without strength but, because of time, he moved slowly. His eyes, though, sharp as when he came into this world. Eli always kept a great tan and observed the people passed out in the afternoon sun, those playing with the Frisbee and the toddler making a sandcastle with their parent. Hot and humid, the air hazed up and down the beach in each direction. Every night he got a different sunset for free. Nature, cheaper than therapy, he thought.

Being in the gardens, a therapy all its own. Still and present and that description also applied to Eli, quiet and calm. Eli didn't bother people and didn't make things about himself and his relationship with the plants included a wide variety of characters. All kinds of life remained at his disposal. Banyans, bamboo, live oaks, palms, mangroves, succulents and wildflowers. There also stood a butterfly garden, a fragrance garden, an edible garden, and a Koi pond. All next to the southwest Florida bay.

This place welcomed the international attention of scholars and plant enthusiasts. The effect of being around all that plant life, that it helped people to be calm and still. Only a stone's throw apart, it almost was impossible to have such two contrasting environments next to each other like the beach and garden. The Child's Rainforest Garden remained his favorite part of the whole property. People ate lunch, take tours and got married, a place for the community and the person.

His mind switched back and forth between the how people appeared on the beach and how they appeared in the gardens. Technology sped them up. People became more disconnected from nature because of their phones and technology. Technology made life fast and convenient. Over time it became more and more sophisticated while nature changes form. Sometimes mother nature roared up the coastline and would disrupt life and its' inhabitants.

Eli loved life and he enjoyed seeing the 170,000 people that came every year to the gardens for events, conferences, meetings, receptions, and weddings. Over 800 people a year volunteered and 8600 children visited each year. Plants and life lived interdependent. Eli treated all the plants kindly and spoke kindly to them all. Whether the succulent or an orchid, Eli enjoyed a personal and silent relationship with each. Eli, alert and aware didn't ever need anything. He chose this place because of so much life. Pain averted from his body and, comparatively speaking, he remained healthier than people his age. Every day became like a new ballgame for him.

With so much variety in the botanical gardens in a typical day, he would be in the rain forest, the succulent desert garden, the lawn, the gazebo and the wedding pavilion. In the mangroves, he would be either in the tropical or coastal section. A lagoon overlooked the bay and children played in the butterfly garden. The whole place remained a spa for the body, mind, and spirit. People rejuvenated and connected to nature apart from the fast and loud pace of modern-day life. Life slowed at the gardens ever vibrant at a level unobserved by the eye.

Eli was aware that people had changed over the years. The way he put it, was that folks had become course in their discourse. In general, he was aware that America was not as quiet as it used to be, not as still. People had become more distracted and materialistic. With a rapid increase in knowledge and in the ability to communicate, people had changed. Though not in their spirit, he thought, as he listened to the cicadas in the oak tree above him. Although they were more active at night, that day the cicadas were in full concert. In the hazy heat, he looked up at the light blue sky, and appreciated the shade of the tree. He heard a plane lumbering overhead and then a noisy car with a big muffler racing down the street nearest to the garden.

With such a massive increase in people's ability to communicate and learn, access to information rapidly increased. Eli thought it made it more difficult for people to stay in touch with their divinity. People complained more and this mystified him because with such an abundance in the country of food, material items and all they needed to survive. Many used available technology for good and many used it for ways that harmed others or themselves. Since he felt more grounded in nature, he didn't like too much technology.

He saw a wedding rehearsal taking place at the gazebo. The humidity revealed that the people in the wedding party simmered. Among the many charms of the garden, a beautiful mansion on the grounds, a wonderful backdrop for a wedding ceremony. A giant oak tree nearby showcased a romantic scene of epiphytes and luscious orchids. People danced on the patio next to the banyan trees. The children's rainforest garden was an excellent place built for an event or reception and the most favored nuptial site was a pavilion that held up to 1000 people. It afforded breathtaking views of the Floridian sunsets. Nearby the butterfly garden and lily pond completed the enchanting scene. This was a place to visit, learn and celebrate. Whether you were a plant enthusiast or just passing time, this place had something for everyone. Fifteen acres of nature playground with so many visitors a year. Eli was in heaven and loved all the people enjoying the garden. Being in charge of all the plant life humbled him. To him, it was a place of miracles because life was ever-renewing. So much silence here, the language of God. Although the knowledge and pace of the world increased, he moved slowly through the world. He noticed that people would look at him kind of funny or in subtle, odd ways because his stillness was unfamiliar to them. The world and its people were tangential and distracted. All of the nature that surrounded him in the garden and the beach kept him quiet and slow. Nothing was a hurry or late and everything happened when it needed to.

Chapter Two: **The Takeaway**

At twenty-four years old, Trevor wanted his best friend back. He never imagined having to go through Tracy's funeral and sat on his bed with his hands over his face. Then, night after night, he dreamed. Most of the view of the dream appeared veiled and obstructed. He saw gold lights that twinkled like fireflies and resembled stars. What concealed his sight, he wondered? Intuition showed him something mysterious and spellbinding. Like the corner of a cloth that revealed something that transcended waking and life. Then a new wave of grief overcame him. He played basketball with Tracy his buddy and when he first met Tracy, he thought him to be a jerk. Ironic, he thought, how they became best friends. Trevor wondered about the possibility of himself who'd been the jerk. They used to play chess outside in the driveway of Tracy's house. Kiana enjoyed being a homemaker. She still remained a strong Catholic woman with deep religious roots. A very sweet woman, Kiana found herself now cloaked in sadness. Tracy 23, didn't see the truck scream through the traffic.

Though he rarely was with his father as a kid, Trevor occasionally went to church with his mother. Trevor read the book of Revelation out of curiosity and found it to be so dramatic compared to other parts of the bible. Trevor searched parts of the Old Testament, but found it dry, long, and boring. Revelation revealed the end of the world and for everyone who loved Tracy, the world ended. A tsunami of grief washed up on the island of their lives. The splatter caused devastation everywhere. Curiosity being second nature and not so intentional. Technology bombarded him every day about spirituality and consciousness. A new level of awareness surfaced on the planet. So many viewpoints and different perspectives on God. Trevor impressionable as any young adult would be, thought of an Einstein quote that flashed across his mind, "Intellectuals solve problems, and geniuses prevent them."

A new avalanche of grief knocked him down like he stood in the surf of powerful waves. How was Tracy a memory now, a steady person who didn't let things rattle him? They jammed at least once a week together. Trevor worked at the local music store saving enough money to purchase an electronic drum set. Tracy played guitar and they got better with time without any big aspirations. They played a few hours on the weekends. Now he lacked the desire to play the drums.

His curiosity about God stirred for a while. He loved to watch videos on YouTube about God and consciousness. Many questions hung in his mind about God and he longed for an understanding about what direction was right to him. Tracy's mom hung pictures of Jesus and Mary in their house. A canyon of the unknown stood before him. He came back to the present. Usually he would play the drums along to music on his headphones. Trevor hooked up his drums up to his amp or the headphones, which made the drums stealth like. He loved the amp because of the power, vibration and sheer noise. Not many people knew that he loved spiritual music as well.

God a great mystery to Trevor, possessed a sublime presence. Jesus, a prophet to some, the Word to others, part of the Trinity, God himself or an amazing teacher to others held many titles. So many people with so many different viewpoints. Trevor liked the idea of Jesus being God because he needed a person to relate to. The enormity of God was not be understood by a human mind. He didn't know why God allowed this to happen to Tracy, to his family and to him. Reflection took the center of his mind.

Videos on YouTube about the end of time or the second coming of Jesus passed him by as he browsed through all the music he wanted to listen to. What about the people other than Christians when Jesus came back? Would they all go to hell? What about all the people who lived before Jesus? How were they to be saved when Jesus wasn't even on earth yet? The depth of those questions left him perplexed at the same time. Not everything on the internet was true and he didn't want to do get caught up in it.

Trevor remembered the music store and sampling some new and used electronic drum kits. In the store people banged on things in the percussion area, practiced on guitars in the guitar area and sung through new mics and amps. Invigorated and excited, he borrowed some drum sticks by the counter to play for a while. He noticed a tattoo on an employee's arm. Musicians often sport tattoos as a subculture thing; though again people in all groups these days sported tattoos. He viewed a remarkable one and he commented on it. He couldn't help but admire the quality of the work seeing only what might be the face of Jesus. The employee behind the counter told him so. Then lifted up his sleeve more which allowed him to observe the face of Mary with a strikingly beautiful face. The man told him it came from the Pieta by Michelangelo in the Sistine Chapel. He brought up how there were two main beliefs in the world now. Not the topic that comes up in a music store. There was so much crossover in religions. The dude told Trevor that his dad died and he went through a period when he partied hard and hated God. However, Jonathan his name, said he found solace in Jesus and Mary especially in the lows where he didn't want to live anymore.

Trevor associated that tattoo with Tracy's death, a reminder that Jesus is with us and does not forget us. Our understanding of God broadened because of physics and metaphysics. We had been on a massive upward learning curve in regards to the universe. The words consciousness surfaced in as many religious terms like Jesus, Mary, Judaism and Pentecostal. The latter group spoke always about sin, evil and the end of the world. The Book of Revelation being incredibly dynamic with no way in his mind to pin down the timing of events. He remembered the images of Revelation, like the "the woman clothed with the son" and "the dragon" and the face of Jesus "shining like the sun." Too much to think about. Life, as much mystery as truth. Why did God allow this?

Trevor knew he would never get another friend like Tracy. They were friends since high school. He remembered sitting in chairs in Tracy's driveway playing chess. They had been competitive at chess, basketball, frisbee and pool. Trevor played a little better at chess, Tracy a little better at basketball. Playing pool, a draw. Trevor planned to go to Tracy's house that day to check on his family. The home remained familiar and full of religious symbolism; a beautiful crucifix, lovely images of Mary and The Divine Mercy print of Jesus. Instead of driving him away from God, this tragedy set him on a personal search and path with many turns.

He didn't know that Kiana and he were alike. She acted like a mother to him, and Trevor, a young male, searched for ways to expand his life. She continued to be devout, spiritual, religious and humble. An eternal Presence around her intrigued him. Her family, from Hawaii and had been stalwart Catholics and his family not otherwise specified Christian. Trevor's faith diverged from formality and deep inquisition. Kiana faced life's challenges. Trevor, questioned and tried to find a spiritual niche. It was hard for each of them to spiritually stand up. A deep connection had been uprooted like a big oak tree struck by lightning. Trevor caught up in idealistic prophecy and didn't like too much religious drama. The end of the world was the last thing on her mind.

Chapter Three: **What in the World?**

If the end of the world approached and Jesus' return near, what would happen to all the people who didn't believe in him? Trevor plunged into bible prophecy like a child going through a toy chest. Everyone had a different view of God. Trevor, not aware of end time religious doctrine from other traditions, envied those who had religious or spiritual experiences. You cannot manifest what you want, you can only manifest what exists within you. If you believe the kingdom of heaven lives within you, can you not manifest the kingdom of heaven? Is the kingdom of God within us? Trevor thought about the book of Revelation, the part about the new Jerusalem coming out of the sky. If the kingdom of God exists within, how does it descend out of the sky?

He had understood "seek ye first the Kingdom of Heaven and all this shall be added to you." Like put off all your pleasures, be super good, pray like crazy and then maybe God will give you what you want. However, he began to believe that stepping out of the way made life easier if you allowed for the things in your heart to take place. Wanting puts us in a place of suffering because we don't possess something. Putting God first allows those important things to come to us. Would a big giant war like Armageddon occur or some kind of transformational change? Would people become more spiritually aware because of the answers that science gave us about how everything looks connected at physical, metaphysical, molecular and spiritual levels? Are spirit and matter intertwined and we try to figure things all out? Why would Marian apparitions occur as they have? Warnings came of chastisements because God "had enough" of what people did to the earth and to each other.

The rain pelted the window as he listened to Hymn of the Cherubim on You Tube. Soothing. Did Jesus go to another planet and did they need to be saved? Trevor thought out of the box. Are we made to worship God or the One Creator of everything we see and don't see? Creation looks all too big for us to be the only ones. Too much to figure out and we're kept in a bubble despite many advances in modern science. We constantly scan the stars looking for life and taking amazing pictures that reveal how small we remain. Yet, we read in the bible that each one of us remains important to God. How can he keep track of everyone? Trevor thought Jesus helps us make sense of God. No real way exists to understand the enormity and power of God. What drives consciousness and awareness? Einstein said he wanted to know the mind of God and all else was details. Are consciousness and awareness the mind of God ?With only five senses, we barely pick up anything with that.

Trevor hoped that reincarnation to be only an idea and wouldn't want to come back and sign up for despair. If reincarnation, then why exists a heaven and hell? You keep coming back in different forms or beings endlessly throughout generations? This was not appealing to him at all. He liked the idea of being with God in heaven and felt Jesus was God who came to earth as a baby. You couldn't get more humble than that. Is our neighbor us? Is that why the bible commands to love your neighbor as yourself? Questions were flying through Trevor's mind. Do you go to heaven when you die or wait till the resurrection? With so many views, what on earth was really going on?

The Marian apparitions suggest a nearing end time. Is Mary like a mother warning her kids "Hurry up! Get in the house before the storm comes"? Is God allowing her to intervene? Do other people who died intervene in our lives? Trevor knew he didn't have the answers so the more he wondered about what was going on, the deeper the hole got. Trevor thought that America was caught up in materialism and comfort and thought that America's biggest challenge was to connect to the divine and stay connected to our source because we had so many cool things to distract us. He started to investigate a little about different end time scenarios though different faith traditions. He remembered a part in the bible about end times and how knowledge would be increased. Nothing pushed knowledge ahead more than the internet. Everything exists on the internet or ties in somehow with technology.

Eschatology of the world religions opened up this door. He wondered, about some kind of common link within the different viewpoints. Could they all be right? Why would most people not believe in Jesus' return? The Buddhists idea tells that the world will collapse in the 5000 years after the death of

Buddha. The decline of civilization would be society being filled with greed, lust, poverty, violence, ill will and sexual depravity.

Trevor hadn't reconciled the eschatological stories of each of the major religions and looked for one common theme in all of them. Decline mentally, physically and spiritually. Each religion had its' own story. Too much for one person to grasp and to hold in the balance. Keep life as simple as possible even though by nature humans complicated life in a plethora of ways. So, what in the world was going on? What was the truth when endless versions exist? Two people could go to the same church and still maintain minor differences in their beliefs. One person could believe in the rapture and the other one not.

Trevor noticed the world used words like "woke." Was the world, with the help of science and religion or spirituality, merging with a God consciousness? He would investigate this further. Different paradigms jockeying for place among the peoples of the world. Which one was right? Would they clash? Would they merge? Some believe in a generational transformation and others believe in a cataclysmic end. Will God intervene to stop us from destroying everything like a parent breaking up a horrible fight between his kids? Are we becoming more spiritual and materialistic at the same time? Earthquakes, starvation, conflict, and poverty always happened. Are we more aware now because of the increase in knowledge and technology? Or, are these and other things we suffer from intensifying on the planet? He looked up and saw the weather on the computer screen. Five hurricanes lined up in the Atlantic alone. What would those storms do and how many countless challenges would be waiting for people?

Chapter Four: **Am I Not Your Mother?**

K iana lost her husband a few years back and not like Trevor, searched for a spiritual foothold. She attended church her whole life. Sometimes she found it hard to pray. When Bill died, she asked God why his death happened. Images of the Sacred Heart of Jesus and Our Lady of Sorrows decorated her home and comforted her. "Thou shall not worship false images" she remembered from the Ten Commandments. She didn't worship these images and thought it ridiculous to think someone thought she worshiped something in a picture frame. How else can we put God in our limited minds? No one can understand God.

She was comforted to sense Jesus and Mary near her and didn't need to explore the origin of everything. Like someone sunning at a resort pool and all the sun, food and drink they hoped for, she trusted God would provide everything she needed. Somehow, she allowed things to just be. She could tell the right amount of God for her and understood Jesus and Mary went through death and loss too and she related this to her own life. Now, through this particular storm, she needed to go inside and couldn't go out to the pool. Too much wind. Too much rain and too many dark clouds. Jesus and Mary remained her spiritual shelter.

Kiana demonstrated an amazing amount of grace when she thought of Trevor. For now, she didn't feel she would reach out to him and couldn't even pray and all her friends at church, only a text or call away. People supported her because they loved and wanted to help her. At the rosary and the funeral, people gave her overwhelming support. A part of her, however, she would show no one.

Now her husband died years ago and and she surfaced at the resort pool of life again having a long vacation from any sort of grief. She worried about her son and missed her husband in a way only a widow would understand and remembered what the Virgin Mary said in her apparition to Juan Diego. "Do not be troubled or weighed down with grief. Do not fear any illness or vexation, anxiety or pain. Am I not your Mother? Are you not under my shadow and protection? Am I not your fountain of life? Are you not in the folds of my mantle? In the crossing of my arms? Is there anything else you need?"

This enabled her to move forward, one step at a time. She understood Mary would take steps together with her and wished to be with the blessed Mother, as her heart addressed her. She thought about going somewhere where people saw apparitions of the Virgin Mary and considered going to search for an apparition, but unsure it to be a wise use of money. She once overheard a priest at an appreciation dinner at her church say he didn't believe any of the apparitions to be anything more than just apostasy.

Kiana became very fragile and strong at the same time and experienced Mary showing up on her radar in the most subtle ways. An image in a store of Our Lady, a rosary decal on the back of a car and the obvious statues in church. The internet contained those images. However, this searching occurred inside of her as inner purpose.

She always spoke the truth and all she wanted to talk about after Tracy's death was her pain, but not enough money in the world existed to pay someone to listen to her. Nor did she want to put all the grief on her friends. No one else extended that amount of graciousness. Invaluable gems, her friends remained there for her. Her friends and family, a safety net for her. The only direction to turn was inward to the ever-present One and she turned to Jesus and Mary. All her heart was yearning. Kiana had energy, devotion, took action and was being transformed. Body, mind, emotion, and energy. With all of this, she poured herself into the divine.

Chapter Five: **You Won't Believe This**

R on sat in the restaurant and looked out of the window in silent bitterness. His friend Al met him earlier for a drink, as they did once or
twice a week. Al and his wife went to church and seemed as well adjusted
as anyone. Although he went to church, he didn't come off as religious or
"churchy." He didn't impose his views on others.

Ron, being gritty and skeptical deep down wanted to believe in God
during his rough life. Sports, his past time, not God or religion. Much of
his time he absorbed whatever might be on television. With so many channels now, he thought, the more channels the worse television became. It
kept him occupied at night. Ron felt content to just be lonely, but he would
never admit it. Open to a relationship although never seemed to meet the
right girl. Some attractive with great personalities, but all of the pieces not
in place, for him. Ron, fifty-five and searching while buzzed on bourbon
looking at the museum of his mind. Staying home, he'd zone out with wine.
Although he drank alone, sometimes, he justified it by telling himself that
he wasn't drinking much and didn't drink a lot and drive.

Ron's mind like the Louvre, full of images. The images from his past
and his future. Silent with white noise around him in the form of conversations or sports on television. Like he walked through an endless hall of
images. On the left, images from his past and to the right, images from the
future. The images passed in his mind of being abused as a child by a relative, the mistakes he made, the money he wasted and the chances he didn't
take or let go. The other side, what he longed for, to be able to be more
creative, to not be sad, the places he wanted to go, the money he wanted to
make and what he wanted to be true.

Ron coveted how Al seemed to be so at peace with life even though
his wife just survived breast cancer. Al shared with him how hard the dif-
ficulty of seeing her go through that and how much his view of life and his
marriage changed. Every moment, a divine instant that he would try not

to waste. Ron's faith waned between skepticism and hope. He knew many people experienced harm in the Catholic Church and could see it as corrupted, diminishing its' credibility. He remembered seeing that awful wreck on the news near where he used to live. A car and a person inside smashed by a driver who drove off still on the run. Everyone wondered what happened to that person who drove away in a panic, terrified that they hurt someone. Their conscience a torment.

In his home, a little mirror on the wall displayed the Ten Commandments on it. Ron would pass by it just to see how he looked and used to know them by heart. A Jewish friend, even a bigger sports freak than he gave it to him. Sports bonded us together by the masses. Your team, my team, their team and people hating others only in fun. Fun. A distraction from life. From our jobs, routines and things that made us suffer or from the things that challenged us. Ron viewed religion in a similar way; but, people killed each other over it even to this day. Why? So much imposing of one's beliefs on others going on. The best thing he thought that religion offered, freedom from ones' self, loneliness, and solitude.

Ron and Al just finished off a basket of wings and fries. They always shared the same 25 piece wings. Medium hot with fries. They stared at the golfers on tour and, if they were good, could make a ton of money. A short story about how much money the best golfers made aired on the television. Somewhere between 30 and 115 million dollars. Ron wanted Al's life and envied him because of the closeness of he and his wife and children. And, he wanted to make the money that golfers made. Just playing golf. No work in that unless you held a different perspective. Ron wanted to go home. The hard part, he would be alone and scrolled through his phone and absorbed music, exercise, finance, teaching and health food videos that were just endless. He looked down and observed a lady's face looking up. The name on the video title line, Messages in Medjugorje. The woman looked up with what looked like tearful joy on her face. Alcohol, became a lousy companion.

Chapter Six: **Thou Shall Not Steal**

On the run and running out of time, Quinn left the scene of the accident and the police looked for him. If he went to the hospital in a nearby town, he would be caught. Quinn drove the old Chevelle, but both the driver and the car appeared heavily damaged. The police looked everywhere for him and his leg looked bad.

Quinn couldn't shake a complicated past and remembered stealing as a little boy. It made him edgy. He also stole because his parents rarely bought him anything he wanted and didn't have much time for him. His parents drank and fought and those moments made up most of his vivid memories. So many times when they slept during the day. They say when people die or when relationships end, you remember the good times. This couldn't be the case for Quinn because the gloomy days outnumbered the good.

Growing up, he related to the kids who got into trouble. The only time he had adrenaline, when he did the wrong thing. For the most part, he made bad grades and rebelled. Now he did something terrible he meant not to do. This, an accident and his mind circled in a frenzy.

His conscience bared down on him now like a kamikaze pilot barreling down toward a battleship. His arm and foot were broken. His conscience told him he did something wrong, and his body shouted at him in pain knowing he should go to the emergency room.

In his household, as he grew up with few boundaries. When his parents drank, the boundaries shifted all the time. His parents would holler. They would say no. They would be lush and would hurt him and hurl insults at him before passing out. The train tracks of emotions switched often though he didn't know in which direction. Like walking across a driving range, sooner or later, you'd be hit. He became unpredictable, impulsive and reckless, like them. Quinn understood this instinctively and the poison in his parents' minds became his own.

Quinn needed help though he would be arrested if he went to the hospital. How could he ask God for help? Would God listen? As a kid, though, Quinn had asked God for help and God answered. As a tormented and desperate teenager, he kneeled and begged for help. At school he sought out the best person to talk to. Her name, Ms. Bryant shined as his his favorite teacher. She worried about him and could see the wear and tear on his face at school. She once sent a note home with him, but the note never made its way to his parents. Afraid they would blow up because a teacher cared about him. He lied and told her he gave them the note. She suspected foul play and wondered about getting involved. Eventually, she did become involved. The school counselor called him into the office to check on him.

All hell broke loose. Everything changed. He remembered the chain of events. The teacher and counselor spoke to him in the office. The same day, a social worker showed up at the school and then late the same day, the social worker went to his home. His mom, already drunk and his dad hadn't gotten home from work, yet. He went to a shelter and his parents avoided being arrested, but the state became involved in their lives. They received a service plan, parenting classes, outpatient substance use classes, counseling and drug tests regularly. On top of all of the bad feelings, Quinn carried a terrible sense of guilt. Quinn believed he hurt and fractured his family.

Quinn remembered when Child Family Services got involved, he fell into a hornet's nest of negative emotions. He wanted all the hurt to go away, but the situation changed as child services moved them to safety. He didn't want his parents to get mad at him but he could not avoid it. He didn't want to go to a strange place like a shelter. He didn't get the parents he dreamed about. He loved his parents and wanted them to stop drinking and being violent. He wanted his parents to be loving and nurturing. Not intense and intrusive.

Eventually, his parents continued down the same dark path they'd been on. They lost custody of Quinn and his brother. The foster family, good enough, his connections with them no more than tentative. He went to go to therapy once a week for a long time and remembered the counselor as a nice person who always gave him a snack. Why wouldn't things go right? Now, the worst jam of his life. Life caved in on him like being in the bottom of an hourglass as he accepted, surrendered and let go.

Terrified and in pain he drove to the hospital and then again, his life changed dramatically. A voice inside his spirit urged him to "ask." He pulled up to the hospital and passed out. Inquisitive medical staff peered through the front doors of the hospital and observed the banged-up car. Alerted by law enforcement, they looked for an injured person involved in a hit and run accident. Quinn remembered seeing people rushing to his car and as he lost consciousness.

Chapter Seven: **The Sheep Are Asleep**

The number of things came to him on his phone leaves one spellbound. Trevor possessed the same handheld computer as everyone else. Look up restaurants, read news articles, book flights and learn from gurus, at any time and his phone became familiar with his tastes. Trevor received more junk emails than his mom did actual junk mail. Everyday came new information. Knowledge increased exponentially. Technology grew smarter and more powerful and held the ability to run our lives. What contended with technology more than nature itself? Life became artificial as if technology photo bombed nature.

The world became a different place now. Trevor tried to imagine life thirty years ago and being a newshound, held a surprising interest in politics. His phone encouraged him to get out and vote for this person and he remembered when only a few sources generated news. A few windows through which humanity became a skyscraper of windows with an enormous amount of vantage points. He couldn't help but see how advanced we became while at the same time see a decline in American society. People became so reactive. Complaining at an all-time high. Yet, we enjoyed more luxuries than ever before. Trevor wondered if the more materialism, the worse off we became.

Technology made miraculous breakthroughs in science, medicine and other fields. Riots like in the 1970s reoccurred and became much more widespread. With political correctness, everyone got offended over everything and took everything so personally. Religion and spirituality became intertwined in a conflicted tryst of morals and the attitude anything goes. He remembered someone uttered what once wrong is right and what once right is now wrong. Can we look at life simply like a giant grey area where the spiritual battles on the planet took place? Trevor thought anti-establishment took place in the 1960s and 1970s. Now you couldn't be against anything or speak out about anybody.

So many people in so many positions of power got into trouble for lack of integrity. Numerous news stories grew about politicians and other leaders committing fraud, embezzlement and things like sexual misconduct. People didn't respect the President or the office. As long as the economy did well, they remained okay with who lived in the White House. Leadership and the lack thereof weakened the fabric of our society. Technology and the human race became ever more sophisticated and changed all the time. God, however, the same all the time. Life had become more intense, fast and superficial. Folks didn't even leave their homes to go to counseling anymore. Media outlets sided one way or another. People, addicted to their phones, responded and enjoyed a bewildering amount of choices of things to do. So many jobs and careers went under because of machines. Most people didn't object because their lives became easier, on the whole. However, the kicker for him, becoming dependent on something not natural, but on something man-made.

America losing its wholesome appeal. Not a popular view, but you couldn't speak out. So somehow society took relative truth to shame by trying to make other people feel bad if they had different beliefs.

Judgment, he thought, always kept our minds off of God. On the one hand, the annihilation of consciousness by technology crept in. Trevor had talked to so many people about the very topic. So overwhelming and prevalent and thought life would eventually be a return to nature because, with the preponderance of technology, we would become disconnected from others, from ourselves, from life and from God.

Indifference towards others and to ourselves increased. We looked for our gain. Hate crimes, rampant and spreading as American society plummeted like the Hindenburg. The world entered spiritual identity crisis as materialism increased. Somehow, people moved to spirituality more than religion. East and West cross-stitched because of the internet and one's ability to learn. Gurus on YouTube who said we experience everything only from our five senses so the world is experienced differently from one person to the next. The idea of universal consciousness is not new. Trevor wondered if the world expressed itself in a large variety of ways and if we are all part of consciousness. His father never weighed in on the debate until he had become older and now had an injury. His answer when asked why he had a bible, "you never know." "Nothing is wrong with life itself" he heard another guru say. "People mess things up." "You either realize you are God or a poor little me," said another. Those statements mystified Trevor.

It's hard to tell what's true. Are the government and media behind the control of the masses of humans on earth? Is the truth relative? Or, is one truth manifested in many forms? Jesus said, "I am the way, the truth, and the life." So then is the Tao Jesus? Because the Tao is the way. His mind exploded with questions. Sorting through all the answers, a life's work. The greatest nation on earth is privileged, progressive and free. Are we all like sheep being controlled by commercialism and markets? Sheep of the world asleep? Or, spiritual sheep awake and listening? This metaphor worked for him.

The world boasted tremendous inventions. Technologically speaking, we grew exponentially. Will we become weaker as computers become stronger and more capable? They don't sleep, are fast remember everything. Are all religions entertainment about God? Somebody recently implying religion is 99.9% about not dying.

Trevor, a thinker, but he liked music too. An Einstein quote referred to needing only a chair, a violin, and a table with fruit. Life is music, he remembered someone else saying he and Tracy used to have these talks about life and religion. Everybody had the Book of Revelation imprinted on their mind. The unspoken end of the world mystery no one had ever figured out. God meant to be a mystery for a reason. People spoke about how if you wanted to destroy America from within, technology and addiction would be a pretty good start. In current America, addiction became rampant. If America got addicted to technology, it would be lethal, he thought.

On the other hand, advances in technology and life were helping make people's lives easier and healthier. Maybe we need protection. With all this hype about consciousness, the world was becoming more spiritual but religion had less of an impact. What about religion and all the wars based on religion? The idea surfaced in his head was that two paradigms exist in the world. One was, God and us. The other, we are God. In many ways, society was like a big giant ego with an underlying and separate component, the spirit.

Technology pushes us away from one another and we are less human and more like machines. More and more children are on the spectrum of autism. Common among them is the challenge to communicate with each other. We have less trust in our government and are becoming dehumanized. Technology has a will and consciousness of its own. The line between reality and fantasy had become blurred. Virtual reality allows people to play in different worlds. Cars are becoming self-driving.

Trevor remembered reading an article about how aliens from other planets were among us. The world would freak out if this were true. Were we all blissfully unaware of subliminal messages beaming out of television and various electronic devices? Media distractions bombard us and we are being lulled into complacency. What would the angle be? To be controlled and bounded? Was money our God?

Trevor remembered something about Einstein saying the right answers are not so important as the right questions. Seems we are being numbed to sleep and are conforming. We haven't had a strong leader in so long, he thought. People don't look up to our leaders like they did before and at the same time, no one seems to be questioning authority. We watch television and we don't have to have an imagination because technology does it for us. The whole culture seemed to be in decline.

Why wouldn't we be easy to control? If we are citizens who don't think for ourselves, obey without question, are submissive, don't think outside of the box and are content to sit back and be entertained, we are easy to control. Was there an invisible order sustaining and controlling apparent freedom? Trevor was thinking of the country he had grown up in as he watched changes taking place.

Trevor looked up at the twilight sky as he finished his ten-mile run. It was cold outside and the way his mind processed when he was jogging was different than any other time. He was aware he was not the only one who was thinking this way. Are we God he thought? A man he met once asked him a question. "Is the water in the fish the same as the water outside the fish"? The man asked. "Yes" answered Trevor. Still, in his mind, he wondered how could we be God?

Chapter Eight: **Do They Want Us To Be Afraid?**

R on sat at the bar stalling going home. A big vacuum occupied his life with no one there. He saw the television screen. The shootings took place across the nation increased as the new terrorism. America harming itself. Bombs going off at concerts and random shootings became common. Stories surfaced about gun control. Are we an angry nation? Did a moneyed few people use us as expendable resources? Society became more unstable. The government stepped into the issues more and more. Did they want us afraid for some crazy reason? To Ron, we became more distrustful of each other. He thought bitterly of the failure of his marriage and of how he only could be with his kids every other weekend. He harassed himself by harsh self-judgement and watched the television report, regarding the question does the U.S. government represent the majority of American citizens? He remembered those who have not lived their life think more about the end of time and they are more afraid of the end compared to those who live their life to the full. His unlived life pointed into the direction of the end. A study recently released showed the government became ruled by the rich and powerful or an economic elite. Therefore, the policies of the government favor special interests and lobbying groups.

Only a few people are ruling the world and are we on the way from oligarchy to fascism where private corporate interests rule and money calls the shots. Ron thought about the astronomical amount of money needed to get elected. Congressman enjoy access to connections and information to increase their wealth in ways unparalleled in the private sector. Ron thought to himself we became corrupt, possibly to the point of no return. Getting elected seemed to him to be political bribery wherein the political system caved into major contributors in a way, they want and expect favors after the election is over. Jaded and pessimistic, he wondered if all the news polarized as the left or the right.

Ron wouldn't be surprised if America become a fascist society. Congress would be in session and people would get elected and the media would cover politics, as usual. The consent of the public would not matter as much. The oligarchic elite would control the government behind the scenes. He thought oligarchic corporatism wherein moneyed interests ruled over the people. The American government by design is to be a democracy or republican form of government. The government is top-down and one developed into a totalitarian regime like ones in the past police states.

How could America turn into this? How could people be duped? Ron thought America became lulled to sleep by technology and addiction. When young, he used to spend all his time outside using his imagination. The media perpetuated fear in many stories about terrorism. Now the police became the bad guys, the neighbors became bad guys and so on. Did we need to be afraid of so many things or are we being programmed to do so? Everyone gets all their information on the phone now. Living alone, he spent lots of time to reflect and ponder.

Ron found himself watching one of those news stories. American social scientists did some research on the American populace. The results indicated Americans became more likely to die from heart disease than from a terrorist attack and more likely to die from an airplane accident rather than a terrorist event on a plane, more likely to die from a car accident than a terrorist attack and more likely to die by a police officer than a terrorist. Are we then becoming slaves without knowing ? Domestication seemed like easy as long as the American people possessed their cell phones and the internet. America didn't seem strong now. Now fearful, pacified and controlled.

Ron wondered if he was being negative because things in his life had not gone well. There was the divorce and his kids older now and who didn't seem interested in seeing him because of being busy with their jobs and friends. Sometimes he felt despondent, but managed to motor through. Everyone was on their phones all the time in traffic. Life was becoming easier to manage in an endless variety of ways because of technology. Everyone talked about the irony of being able to communicate at the drop of a hat, but technology entertained and wowed us so we personally connected less and less.

People always had their heads down. Ron thought that was such a peculiar phenomenon. For most of his life people had held their heads up. Now, they looked down at their screens when they crossed the street or sat across the table from one another. We're separated because we're looking at our devices. He remembered some bible scripture indicating knowledge would be increased as a sign of end times. America is like a zombieland with everyone addicted to technology. What is the temperature in any part of the world? Convenience is king.

What do we do? The rate at which technology is increasing is exponential. The reporter talked about a study where Americans view so many hours of television a month. Televisions, laptops, personal computers, and cell phones changed American life and he knew he could not keep up. One psychologist interviewed on the show said if there is an addict in the house, everyone in the house is an addict. We are addicted to technology similar to drug addiction. People associate tension relief with watching television. The research also indicated brain waves slow down and transform people into a more passive and non-resistant state. According to a study, the reporter stated prisons are now using television to keep the inmates quiet.

Television is controlled by mega-corporations and the corporate elite. What is controlled by the corporate elite? Ron thought. They referenced Edward R. Murrow from the 1958 speech he gave in which he'd said we are wealthy, fat, comfortable and complacent. He went on to say television is being used to distract, delude, amuse and insulate us. People are content to remain controlled. To Ron people had been lulled into a trance and had become indifferent to others. Racial injustice was growing and seemed like people made enemies of each other more so than ever. He thought America was in a silent war. The war was taking place in courtrooms, streets, public offices, classrooms, in towns and cities across America.

Chapter Nine: **Life Without God**

T he news showed the driver of the car who killed her son, Tracy, to be in police custody. The report said he drove himself to the hospital and collapsed on arrival due to injuries. She wondered who would do such a thing as a hit and run, especially when someone died. Life, a journey ended quickly for her son. The world says you are grown up when you are twenty-one, but to Kiana, her kid would always be her kid. He stayed out of trouble, worked and loved his girlfriend. An unfamiliar rage she felt. She tried to find a way to find out who killed her son. Overwhelmed, she froze like a container with an unremovable lid. Faced with this tragedy and consumed by sorrow, unlike God to be elusive.

For Kiana, life held a serious purpose at the end, which is to die and go to heaven. But, what about those like her son who were getting started? People followed the same traditions as their parents. Tracy, a typical kid, did go to church with the family every Sunday. Unlike his best friend, Trevor, he didn't question everything.

Tracy didn't worry about the end of the world. She remembered her son telling her, though, how much he and his best friend talked about life. The obvious topic, the dramatic and encrypted Book of Revelation no one to figure out. Trevor kept a voracious appetite for reading at a young age and loved spiritual philosophy and theology. Were we put here by aliens? What about all these Hindu Gods? How come the sayings of Jesus and Buddha were so similar? The big question he asked, is there God and us or are we God? At first, she thought it to blasphemy to assume we are God. In modern times a new language asserted consciousness equals God. When she grew up, people didn't talk about consciousness. Privately, it had merit while she held on to her faith.

Believing in God gave her a future and not believing in God took that future away. Kiana's greatest desire and aspiration, heaven. Kiana concluded without God, the universe is doomed for that matter. She never believed the universe created itself and didn't believe the grave to be the end. Her heart believed Tracy to be in heaven. The only thing to give her consolation and intuitively understood she would not be able to make it unless she had faith. It had carried her through everything and she had been a devout Catholic her whole life. What stood in front of her looked bleak. Heaven promised hope. For her, no threat of non-being.

Kiana liked Trevor's enthusiasm to find God. Not Catholic, he still had a spiritual fervor beyond simple faith. No one understood what it would be like after non-being. To her life was not an absurd accident. Seen and unseen. The basic elements of God. The mystery of God left her thinking. She kept reading her Jesus devotional that reminded her to meet Him in the now though she wanted to be with him in the future.

A foggy morning and her favorite noise, silence. Sometimes she found some gentle spiritual music on the internet that soothed. She drank her coffee and she sat with life. The house in which she and her family had lived for years, now empty, except for her. Although, losing loved ones challenged her meaning, value and purpose. The briefness of life pressed against her and as she now became older, the imminence of the end of her life almost seemed to surround her. Nothing would matter in a million years and nothing in a million years matters now. Now, the keyword. Her devotional stressed presence and the present. She remembered to meet Jesus in the present moment and be aware of His presence. The path, now, not behind her and not in front of her. She wondered how she mattered to God being a speck in the entire universe and believed she mattered to God. When little, she feared losing her parents. Her mother died when she was in her 30s and her father when she turned fifty. She lost her beloved husband. Losing her son so suddenly became the most unexpected loss. Grief-stricken, she sat staring into space.

Kiana had heard someone say life would not mean as much if it didn't end. To God, she thought, our life must be like a quick spark and we spend so much of time worrying. In this life, she would not want to live forever. In the afterlife she did and wondered not about whether or not she would be happy and with her loved ones, but what they would do for an eternity in heaven. God's plans she thought. In the big picture comparing our size with that of the universe life she thought to be meaningless and she remembered God has the hairs on her head numbered. Would life be absurd if we lived forever here on earth she wondered? Does it not matter life lasts 70 years so much as what happened in those 70 years?

What about all the things people left undone because they died suddenly? Maybe their life seemed absurd if it ended short and would it seem absurd if they finished all they had to finish?

What however about the absurd life of someone who mistreated someone else? She couldn't think Tracy's life to be absurd. She leaned on the Blessed Mother, as she called her. Her image, before her on the wall in her bedroom bestowing calm and peace at the moment. She believed Mary had gone through her grueling torture as a mom watching her son die a criminal's death at such a young age. Did his death rob his life of meaning? Lighthearted and easy going, Tracy misbehaved like any other kid but stayed out of real trouble.

We live, earn money to pay for clothing, housing, fun, entertainment, food and sustain ourselves from year to year supporting our family and pursuing careers. To what end she thought? At times an elaborate journey leading nowhere. Anyone could say life to be pointless though we do things like take aspirin for a headache, admire the work of a painter or stop a child from putting his hand on a hot stove.

Private reflection became one of her favorite past times. She wondered how paradise could not be tedious and thought God had it rigged so bliss and peace were the only experiences. We are always trying to make sense of the world. Of course, people have thought tedium and absurdity could be part of immortal life. We choose the things we do because we have a finite life and by second nature prioritize our lives choosing one activity over another. Without a sense of time or finiteness, we could choose to do what we want without any time constraints. There is a certain intensity that goes along with life and we are always aware of running out of time and we only get so many choices.

No matter if we are raising a child, sharing time with a lover, performing a demanding task, or creating thoughts or art, we do so within the constraints of time. Kiana had developed a sense of the divine instant if she allowed herself to be aware enough. If we weren't aware of time, our pursuits would change. Things might become easier or optional. What would be so great about postponing death anyway in the grand scheme of things? How could we understand what the ultimate purpose of everything is? If we understood the ultimate purpose for our lives, we would question it and make it non-ultimate. Would someone ask if this to be the meaning of life if we were beholding a vision of God? What would it have meant for us to have a holocaust and everything else we went through? It's incomprehensible though we try.

Kiana thought often in life the value is in the doing. The reward is intrinsic and the outcome doesn't matter as much. If you are a great athlete or chess player and lose, does that mean your life has no meaning and that it is nothing? No one is going to remember what you do seventy years from now so what is the point of doing what you do now? She believed it to be more about the inside of the person than the outside because the experience is only in the present moment. Life isn't about outcomes.

Kiana stayed in existential despair. What if the universe is playful? It is too difficult to think this way if you lost a son? God made everything, but He didn't have to and if he made everything, He saw what could and would happen. Looking up at the stars at night sold to her the vastness of creation and her smallness. What about the playful part? Her son loved to play his music and didn't take life or himself too seriously. Creation isn't going anywhere and doesn't have a place at which to arrive. Tracy played the guitar and worked at a grocery store. He didn't play the grocery store and work the guitar and liked jamming and didn't worry about where he was going to end up. When we travel, we are trying to get somewhere and when we play, we are not. She remembered a philosophy class where she learned we are compulsive and purposeful and going faster all the time. If we get to all our destinations and purposes too fast, what is the point of the journey? If the distance between you and your destination is eliminated, both ends of the journey become the same place. Who wants to obliterate travel?

Tracy's music wasn't about the final notes. He smiled when he played. Life is not about the finale, but that's all we think about. His ending, horrific, his life, wonderful. We grow up in an educational system that is about the next thing to do. First grade, second and so forth. In the middle of life, the next thing is coming and one day you realize you have always felt this way. Expectations cheat us out of life because we think of the next thing on the journey, success or failure and heaven at the end. She thought of Tracy one more time before heading off to bed in her quiet home and unsettled heart. You don't know when it is going to end. He didn't worry about it.

Chapter Ten: **Reflection**

Q uinn lay in the hospital bed with significant internal injuries. Too wounded to be on the run and delirious from the painkillers and horrified at causing a fatal accident. He thought about the series of events that summed up his whole life. Numerous child welfare calls on his parents ultimately ended up with him being removed and aging out of the system. He wanted to call his brother afraid of what Ron would think. Half-conscious and half dead, imprisoned and free by his current set of circumstances. His whole life wrought with dread amongst the fleeting moments with his brother and parents. Some memories surfaced of him playing in the yard and his mom reading to him. Sunshine in the yard and running around on a beautiful day like a dream. The bad dreams most people have once in a while as usual, a way of life for him. Life was a constant state of tension.

Quinn walked in his front door from school one day and with both of his parents passed out from drinking. He never found a way to not come home. Freedom became illusory and evaded him. Courage bubbled under the surface. Afterward, his parents acted as if nothing happened. Sometimes they would apologize and make up for their absence by splurging on something to try to make everything alright. Always like a half step of joy to him. He wanted teachers to notice or see something wrong. On the other hand, he remained afraid of anyone finding out what happened in his family. A giant secret of doom. A light burned inside of him. He and his brother went through some horrific things together. For a brief time, things got better for his brother, when Ron got married. But, eventually, his brother became divorced and heartbroken.

Quinn not only sustained internal injuries and a broken leg, he found himself in police custody. He wondered what the purpose of all the chaos would be and thought of it as riding in a car, as a child, never knowing when the driver would drive recklessly. His whole childhood he gripped. There always seemed to be tension and chaos in his life. Fear, most familiar to him. The doctors told him surgery was necessary. His liver and spleen, damaged in the wreck. He sustained several symptoms of internal bleeding like abdominal pain, shortness of breath, dizziness, and blood in his urine. The doctors told him of the risk. He watched his dad have multiple women come to their house with his mom not around. Interludes of peace with his mom, rare, and he remembered she did drugs a lot while being victimized by his dad.

Quinn, in and out of foster homes during his whole youth felt wanted and unwanted by those who fostered him. Abused by one of the foster parents, he checked out emotionally and lost placement at another foster home because his own behavior became out of control. If the placement didn't undo him, he would undo the placement. That attachment would be weaponized against him sometimes. This led to constant anxiety. Anxiety led him to take matters into his own hands to gain some semblance of control while learning to be a master of disruption rather than a slave to chance.

He envied those kids whose parents gave them lives that looked charmed. Prior to the boys' removal from home, CPS workers visited the house three times before doing anything about what happened there. Drunkenness and drug dealing became common in their house. His parents reassured the workers everything to be fine. Quinn, off and on with drug use, eventually pulled away because his childhood memories of his parents' drug lifestyle.

Chaos and unpredictability, so familiar to him, drove him away from people and he would not allow himself to be hurt again. He heard the beeps in his hospital room from all the machines. So tired he wanted to sleep. That would quiet the chaos in his head. Other times, he wanted things other kids got that his parents never bought them. And now this. Quinn believed he was forgotten by God. He fatally hurt someone and this became the lowest moment of his life.

They would be coming soon to take him to surgery and he thought he might not wake up and started to drift. His memory showed him his dad getting so mad at him. He remembered when his mom would talk to him when high. He couldn't connect with either one. He and his brother depended on each other emotionally. School remained hard when everything was chaotic at home. As a kid, he so often dreamed of all of it ending. A nun chaplain came by his bed and smiled at him peacefully. His shame and pain didn't allow him to talk. The Miracle of The Sun book she held in her arms along with a rosary. She visited briefly and introduced herself, but then the nurse came in to begin the prep for surgery.

Equanimity evaded his life. Dealing with a lifetime of heaviness left him with a constant tension and despair. He thought about all the times he tried to forgive his parents in the hope they would change. The change would come, but as a short honeymoon ending fast. Sooner or later one of them turned into silently moody and easily offended. There would be an explosion emotionally, verbally or physically. Some sort of explosion occurred about every three days. He kept his seat belt fastened and his eyes stayed on the driver.

Quinn felt gratitude for the nun chaplain who came by and gratitude for the nurses who took care of him and for the day CPS removed him and his brother from their home. His mind twisted with grief. At times he hated them. After his own experiences with drugs and alcohol, he fell into big trouble with the law. He didn't want to become like them and didn't know if addiction ran in the family or if the drugs became the most accessible way to deal with the pain regardless of genes. Maybe both. Life slammed him up against a wall.

Quinn possessed inherent humility. He liked animals and they took to him. No one showed him how to love himself though. Some people he looked up to. He thought of Ms. Bryant who understood him. Gentle and powerful at the same time. The people who took power over his life, weak, not grounded, coercive and manipulative, and willing to use force, if need be. A battered body with an untouched living spirit inside of him.

He looked for anyone in his life who had integrity. He wanted to play sports and got a couple of chances, but he never played anything for more than a season. Quinn liked working out and got strong. He and his brother used to work out together. As adults, they took different paths. Due to time and distance, they grew apart. His brother, in his twenties, took a job in another town and their relationship began to fade. Quinn became jealous, his brother did got married and had a couple of kids. Then his brother got divorced. He never put together a long relationship with the right girl. His loneliness, a silent disease as his relationships based on nothing more than mutual benefit until they ran out of gas.

Justice headed towards Quinn like a full-speed locomotive. He became stuck in the tracks staring into the headlight of the diesel beast. Now this was the worst trouble in life. Life was smashing him now, but no one showed him how to make friends with life. Trouble followed his family. He assumed the same dark cloud over his parents was now over him. The storm enveloped him and every direction appeared dark and ominous.

Where was the justice in his own life he wondered? An outcome of a story he didn't author. His parents hardly ever got into trouble with all the drinking and fighting. Each of his parents had gotten a DUI. The lush drunkenness, forgetting what happened the night before, the lack of self-awareness and accountability were crazy-making in his mind. His parents were injustice collectors and had acted entitled, like life owed them something.

Quinn and his brother saw every three days they would drink and were alert as a radar detectors. The pop opening and fizz of a beer can was the flame that lit the candle, which burned for a long night. Nothing ordered or made sense when that happened. The terminal justice was when after he and his brother had been taken away by CPS. Still, the vacuum was there. The ability to connect to others, compromised because home was too much of an environment to react to rather than be encouraged in.

He had been to the hospital before, as a kid and remembered seeing the religious type people with pamphlets walking around. Since his life was so tough, when someone was kind to him, kindness was not something he was very familiar with. This lady stood out and placed the book on the table next to his bed. The orange and pink cover, but he couldn't tell what the title was. She left as the nurses had moved her along to prep Quinn for surgery.

The doctors had given him pain killers. If not for the medication, the pain would have overcome him. He hurt everywhere. The police had taken his belongings. He hadn't even filled out any paperwork at the hospital because he became unconscious as medical personnel had taken him in. Getting voicemail, he hung up without leaving a message. They had not spoken for some time. Time and distance had pushed their lives apart. He was ashamed of what he did and didn't want to admit what had happened. However, when he was down in the dumps, his brother had always known what to do. His brother had been there for him. He worried he might not wake up after the surgery, he hoped speak to his brother one more time. Love was all that mattered to him, although so elusive. Like trying to capture a firefly.

Chapter Eleven: **The Call**

R on drove home after having his usual two drinks. He sat at the bar, for a while, after his friend left. The sports and news on the televisions contained mind-numbing distractions from the moment. Besides drinking and watching television, he left to go home alone and the feeling of loneliness began to set in. He saw the evening fog rolling in off the bay and got into his old pickup truck remembering only the din of mindless information he absorbed from his seat at the bar. No one waited for him at home and he would be alone.

Ron talked to his brother a long time ago and became out of touch and he preferred it that way and didn't want to engage in life too much. He trudged through life, uninspired by anything. He moved to Florida and sold cars for some time. Being a car salesman meant working long days. Half of the other salesmen drank a lot. Teenagers now, his kids still depended on their parents for living supplies and occasional direction.

The church became an oasis for him when he went. He went to connect to God though not to others so much. A loner and a men's group didn't interest him. The irony, he connected with people easily when he tried to sell a new truck, but preferred to be left alone at church. People drained him as he put forth his best efforts during the week to nail down his sales. His gratitude toward God became enormous for getting him through a horrible childhood. His parents didn't show him how to be a parent and he became an avid reader and he enjoyed his solitude.

Restlessness and discontent feelings pervaded his days. As a kid, school gave him a great distraction to that he used to his advantage. Ron thought that things could be better at home if he made straight A's. After high school graduation and on his own, he read voraciously. The book he read told him no such thing as permanent happiness existed. We only experience happiness as something momentary based on our five senses whether it be intimacy, great food, music, seeing the beauty of nature or smelling bacon.

Those moments are brief. We suffer when we try to stretch them out past their end. That suffering creates anxiety. The part that he understood the most, the only permanent thing is God. Time he realized to be just an illusion. Everything happens in the moment. Memories and future dreams are nothing more than mind made stories that we think are real. Reality, he tried to understand and to live always in the moment. All the heavy stuff he read fed his curiosity for learning. The more he learned, the more he didn't understand. Maybe not knowing in an odd way, the only way to understand God. The more you pursued it, the more it eluded you. On the surface, his life plain and predictable. The life of God though, underneath him and all around him. Each time he read a book it, helped him look at his life as a different movie. Each book became a filter through which to view his own life. Reading provided a kaleidoscope of angles from which to view life. This made it interesting. An intellectual thirst for knowing God pervaded his being. We have all the underpinnings of God in religious characters from different religions that seemed to all make up the divine family.

Ron drove home and the rain started to pelt the windshield. The night became murky. Both hands on the wheel because he consumed two drinks and wanted to pay attention. Paying attention to life became more intrinsic to him. The church contained its assortment of characters from the priest down to the elderly couple who attended church. New life echoed in the church in the form of a baby, who got everyone's attention. Kids in school who went to church and youth groups, he remembered wanting to catch a draft of what others' lives looked like.

Ron noticed a missed call from his brother. With so many robocalls and bill collectors, he hardly ever answered his phone unless he recognized the contact. His brother's name came upon the call list with no voicemail. They rarely touched base these days. He got home late and didn't want to talk, but something told him to return the call.

Ron tapped the contact showing his brother's name. When his brother called, he needed something or wanted to complain. He didn't want to be needed tonight and just wanted to go to bed and stood in his kitchen looking out at the rain accompanied now by lightning and thunder. The voice that answered, not his brother. Officer Daniels of the Austin Police Department announced himself. Ron's adrenaline went through the roof.

Chapter Twelve: **Is there time?**

H is plane flew almost 600 mph and practically knocked people down getting off the plane and took an Uber to the hospital. From the moment he got the call he caught the first flight out of Tampa to running into the hospital in Austin. He asked what room his brother occupied and tore through the lobby towards the elevators and burst onto the ICU floor. They told him his brother got out of surgery. Understandably, the police didn't want him to pass. Quinn's brother, Ron, entered the room and he took his brother's hand. The surgeon came in and explained to Ron what happened. The machines told him that Quinn's life would not last long. Ron got rushed out to the hallway as the staff tried to save his brother.

For an hour they tried to save his brother whose vitals started crashing. Nothing worked. The grim scene bewildered and gripped Ron. He reminded himself to breathe. The police stood near Quinn's room. All he did, wait and then it was over. The doctor came out and explained to Ron that they did everything. The internal injuries became too much and his body succumbed. He drank no alcohol that night. The police thought that neither Quinn or Tracy revealed being under the influence of anything. Downpours of grief overcame him as they eventually let him into the room to say his last goodbye. The book on the nightstand next to Quinn's bed entitled Miracle of the Sun. With no idea what the Miracle of the Sun was about, that remained the last of his concerns. He witnessed his brother's death. A lady he noticed in the lobby before remained, but didn't say anything. She looked stunned as if she held something invested in all of this. She didn't introduce herself and he didn't want to meet anyone new. He wondered why he needed to speak to her. He thought that she went for someone else in the ICU. They went through so much together being so close. Only time and distanced pushed them apart. Months since they last spoke. And then, the conversation seldom went beyond superficial. Since his divorce, Ron checked out of life and became less engaged than earlier in his life. If Quinn didn't call, he wouldn't be able to see him at all.

Quinn didn't do a formal will. Their parents out of the picture, he wouldn't inform them. Cremation would cost less and he thought no one would even go to a funeral, if he decided to have one. The hospital case-worker approached him to steer him in the direction of a funeral home. They took Quinn's body out of the room. The medical examiner would do an autopsy to discover the cause of death which would be massive internal injuries. As they moved Quinn out of his room one of the nurses handed Ron the book on the table next to the bed. The Miracle of the Sun. Ron's pastime became surveyor of religion and spirituality rather than an active participant. The topic of spirituality, intriguing. The many works of spiritu-al, rather than religious writers, he found to be fascinating. The parameters created by religion posed as sort of a turn-off.

Ron remembered that Quinn got the worst at home. His brother found trouble more than he did. Since childhood, they moved from apart-ment to apartment. Addicts, his parents exhibited a toxic relationship and moved from place to place. What did this book mean though? Did Quinn become Catholic or religious? Did he been search for God? What about the Virgin Mary and her followers? They maintained no mutual contacts so he couldn't cross-reference any information.

Ron wondered why Quinn had the book in the first place. Had he leapfrogged Ron, spiritually. The whole thing, bizarre. Nevertheless, he de-cided to keep the book as he peeled through the pages. Why of all things would his brother pick this book? The idea of apparitions interested him, but he thought of them as more of a Catholic thing.

His focused again rested on the lady in the ICU waiting room. All the rooms remained full and people milling in and out. He looked at her, a solemn look on her face. The people in the ICU had a certain level of comradery because of their concern about someone. She didn't appear to be connected to any of them. The police had Quinn's phone so Ron couldn't look up his contacts and wondered if Quinn had any good rela-tionships at all.

Ron got a hotel room and collapsed on the bed. A whirlwind of thoughts went through his mind. The toxicity of his parents almost al-ways polluted him. He talked about those things a lot with his wife and in their marital therapy that came too late. Ron remembered only a few good Thanksgivings when young. That time of year meant that the likelihood of his parents being intoxicated skyrocketed. He wondered how much of all chaos they'd carried into adulthood and understood why his marriage didn't last. He'd never known what a healthy marriage looked like and envied people who did.

He never had a sense of love, stability or trust and his childhood, a poor prep for marriage. He got married early in life. Sometimes he thought his parents to be insane with the bullying of each other and he and his brother. They came off as controlling and intrusive. This did not discourage him from trying to find love on his own. He tried to make better choices than they did and tried to be loving towards his wife, but she too came from a similar situation.

Reflections from his life and marriage poured through his mind. His parents, aggressive, neglectful, narcissistic, drug-abusing, guilt-tripping and suffocating. They stood as the dominant models he and his brother had. They had left a deep impression on him and he sought out the same patterns in his adult relationships. His wife had been an alcoholic and, after a while, she turned into a much bigger storm. Ron didn't understand he tried to compensate for having an unhappy childhood.

Unconditional love was unknown as his parents' repertoire because their love remained conditional and reflected their self-value. The only experience of love that he and Quinn ever had left them confused and threatened. Therefore, any experience of unconditional love came off as suspicious and odd.

They didn't learn what they should not put up with. Ron's marriage stood out as dramatic and unstable. The rules changed from day to day depending on whether their parents to be high or not. Subsequently, his marriage, characterized as stormy and romantic.

Ron didn't learn to draw lines with others because lines were crossed in his home as his parents eroded his boundaries. Ron and Quinn didn't learn that misbehaving, guilt and tantrums were all unacceptable. They detached from their parents with love, but no longer wanted to be around them.

Ron nor Quinn was never in a relationship where they trusted people. Their home was not stable or constant. At the drop of a hat, his parents were volatile and disapproving. The same things happened in Ron's marriage. His wife often ran off, cussed him out, broke lots of things and behaved like an idiot. Ron wondered if other kids had confusing unstable family lives. They were not allowed to argue or disagree much. Their parents lashed out at them. Ron and his wife argued a lot. His marriage was wrought with implicit threats real and imagined. Quinn experienced the same things in his relationships as well.

The internal judge, the little officer that inhabited their minds made a heyday out of self-criticism. This also stood in the way of their relationships and romantic happiness. They still chased after love. This gave birth to depression, relational missteps and miscommunications in their attempts to connect. Self-condemnation of themselves became a loop in their relationships. How he and his brother never developed an addiction he thought was a miracle even though addiction hung over their childhood like a typhoon. They hadn't recovered from the damage.

He roused himself and was reminded about what to do with Quinn. The lady in the ICU waiting room was on his mind. So many family members of people who were sick in all those rooms. He was too grief-stricken to ask, but her presence stayed with him.

Chapter Thirteen: **Vengeance is Mine**

Kiana clung to her religious parameters with a special devotional area in her house for her bible and worship. She tried to stay on the path as usual as much as she needed a consolation many times now throughout her day. Let go didn't work for her at this moment. Most days she held on and let go. After losing her son so suddenly, she curled in on herself and now her life became as internal as ever. She prayed her rosary finding comfort with Mary who in her heart remained her compassionate mother and mother of our Lord. Safe there as if her soul hibernated.

Kiana loved her devotionals as spiritual stones that she placed around her. Jesus Calling, The Imitation of Christ and My Daily Bread, always available on the menu. The pain of losing her son crushed her, but she held it together. God held her together she concluded. Life, made up of polarities, stood as the world we lived in. Good guys and bad guys, up and down, light and dark, cold and hot, love and hate. The last one, where she found a challenge. Love your enemies and bless them that curse you, the scripture she remembered. It's hard for her to revel up hatred in her heart. She thought of Mary and all the tortures they laid on her son.

Kiana's fury grew in her heart. It would not change a thing. Curiosity drove her more than anything. Who ripped her son's life away from her? Once the police report identified the suspect she immediately came on like the burner on the stove. She thought about finding, attacking the perpetrator and defending her child like a mom trying to fight off a dog trying to bite her kid. It became too late for that. At the same time, she remained terrified because she held no idea what that would bring. She wanted to drive to the hospital to meet this person face to face. Deep down, she remained meek and loving although today she carried a sword.

She gripped the steering wheel with tunnel vision and always did for others and the most she did for herself, her investment of time with God. She got it all back with a great life. Jesus died she thought. The unexpected death of her son, too much for her mind. She wanted to confront some-one and at the same time. Her life seemed together and someone came and tore her puzzle apart. Kiana would be putting it back together one piece at a time.

Going to meet Quinn became the next piece. The whole way to the hospital she gripped the stirring wheel and leaned into the drive. As she viewed the hospital in the distance her breathing became shallow and her blood pressure took to the stars. She wondered if this to be her right for her to do this. What if the guy was injured? Then she thought that if the police caught him, they would never let her to him. She made her way up to the ICU taking every step as if she counted them. It appeared as a crazy intense quiet place with lots of people and people hooked up to machines. Empathy was found nowhere near her though she tried to understand who, why and the how.

Life chose however not going to give her that chance. There became a scrum at the room where Quinn had to be because that one had the cops outside of it. Quinn started to code and die. She sat down in an area near all the rooms. She didn't want to say anything. She just watched it for the longest time. No one bothered her as there with all the commotion and she didn't ask questions. After the longest period, they moved Quinn's body out of the room and a nurse handed Quinn's brother the book that had been by the bed.

She didn't forget what had happened and had to live with this now. She didn't think what happened to be an accident because Quinn left the scene. His parents weren't responsible and they had taught him to not be respon-sible so his first instinct, to run. Kiana needed Quinn to know her suffering as a result of the accident. There appeared no way now to avoid the suffer-ing and deal with the anger. She remembered a quote by Einstein "anger lies in the bosom of fools." Anger resided in her now, not comfortable with it while at the same time feeling entitled to it. This became her Gethsemane. This whole thing made her think of herself more than ever. She became also occupied with Quinn, someone she never heard of until now. She had been thrown to the opposite of what her life appeared to be, solemnity and quiet. She became anything, but quiet on the inside where the storm now resided. She held on to everything she possible so that she would not be stripped away from her sanity. She recovered from her husband's death, but she never made it back completely. A crater in her spirit formed.

Could she move on without going quietly insane? What about Quinn's life? She didn't know anything about him. In her soul, aware that God did not do this to her. Forgiveness, a flash in her conscious mind. She courageously went to the hospital to confront her offender. Justice came swooping down before her arrival so swiftly. Her flight into revenge and confrontation canceled. She didn't see Quinn victimized. Because of the life she led, she succumbed to the idea of forgiveness that looked for room among all the other things in her heart. Quinn's death did give her a partial redemption. The consequences of her son's death became enormous though she had the ability to be compassionate with herself. She went over the consequences of Tracy's death for Trevor and all of Tracy's other friends.

Kiana couldn't expect any restitution for the offense of her son's death. Quinn's death took care of that. If Quinn remained alive it still wouldn't bring her son back. Life gave her pain and consequences. She didn't know how to grieve and how to use her anger to take care of herself. She relied on God, all she had left. Here was a person who had such a great impact on her life and she didn't face him. She judged him as bad because he left the scene of the accident. She wanted God to punish her offender. Because of her character, Kiana thought of compassion and mercy at the same time. She had no way other way to think.

Kiana didn't deal with her suffering and anger. She would not get a chance to express compassion and mercy. She thought about the times in her own life when she needed and wanted to be forgiven. Why had this become part of her purpose in life? She served God still and now wrestled with the idea of never knowing why it happened. Down to one breath and one step at a time. She decided not to say something to the man the nurse handed the book to. Why bother him and impose more suffering on him? They became lost and resigned to their inner life.

Chapter Fourteen: **In My Father's House**

T revor became fascinated by the fact of so many forms, titles, and names for the divine. A spiritual philosopher or rock and roll drummer in the making. He became an archaeologist exploring the different faiths or belief systems. Since the dawn of technology and the internet especially, information increased exponentially. He read articles on quantum physics, oneness, Hinduism, Buddhism, and the list goes on and on. According to Google, he discovered 4200 religions in the world exist. The largest is Christianity followed by Islam. The trend seemed apparent to him, the suggestion we are God ourselves manifesting as all types of life. For Trevor, the question remained are we God or are we not God? If we are God, why did Jesus come to die on the cross? Would God be dying for God? That would not make any rational sense. Are we the ones that created ourselves or did a divine being create us? The cross couldn't be for nothing. However, more and more people believed like Einstein, there is no future or past, only the moment, the present moment and nothing else. What about heaven and hell? He had a hard time believing God would doom someone to eternal flames if they weren't good and had a harder time believing in reincarnation. What about the Hindu and Buddhist stuff? Do they suffer when they die or come back as something hideous? He looked up a chart on world religions which looked bewildering regarding creation, the meaning of life, symbols, myths, practices, and the afterlife. Would we be discovering in the future we are indeed part of the one true God? Some people say nature is God. He read somewhere all of life or life is Jesus smiling. Not one person on earth knows.

Science and religion are collapsing on each other. Trevor liked that explanation more. He remembered some statements by Einstein that science and religion are two languages describing the same things. Science does not hold a monopoly on everything that is in space and the world. Recognizing the world is lived through the experimental, discernment and spiritual experiences. Reason and logic alone will not suffice to describe the universe as achieving a higher level of spiritual attainment that is science and also spiritual. God's creation remained alive and active right in front of him in every form of nature and yet we do not believe. The two paradigms of science and spirituality now complement each other and again he remembers Einstein referring to nature as proof.

Science runs by itself and doesn't need God to manage itself. It doesn't worry about God being a mystical and transcendent being. Science cannot touch the vast dimension of spirituality. To Trevor, God made up all the natural laws, but is not subjected to those laws. Spirituality lies beyond our senses. We are like 5 strings on a guitar and God plays with our senses with the created world. So, who's finger is on the truth? Twelve people can be sitting around the table with different impressions and viewpoints about God.

Science is materialistic in its searches for truth and doesn't appear in the vast domain of spirituality. When we are looking for the truth, we cross the world of senses with the world of spirituality. Can we as people even perceive the truth despite all of our searching? I am the way and the truth and the life came to his mind. We can only control what is in the senses therein lies the boundary of our control. Therefore, spirituality becomes a problem beyond our senses. If we can't control, it's mysterious. To Trevor, this remained a universal goal wherein everyone searched for the truth. All the civilizations from the modern world back to the primitive Egyptians were searching for God and the truth. The universe seems to be described as secluded, self-sufficient and all processes take place in a waveform without any influence by an external factor. Many things he read indicated we live in the world of illusion and God is the one beyond the veil of nature powering the whole thing.

Trevor had such a thirst for the truth to find what reconciles everything in the world. He stayed open to reading Christian, Buddhists, Hindus, Zen Buddhism and so on. At some point we had become scientific in our exploration of the truth and science, not always his most interesting topic. He was one to find abstract concepts more appealing. Science doesn't have metaphysical as a component because of so much subjectivity in perception. Metaphysics paralleled transcendence and science focuses on what can be measured and observed. If God is invisible then what? How can you measure invisible? We can measure what is invisible to the naked eye. Wave and particles. If we can measure what is invisible, are we measuring God? This seems to be the two paradigms evident in the world to Trevor. Are we God or are we not God? If we are God, why did Jesus come and die on the cross?

God would not do that for no reason. The more he looked into the puzzle, the more pieces he found almost as if truth itself was ultimately elusive unless you believed Jesus was the embodiment of truth.

We can't describe the truth of God as an undisputed and verifiable truth or fact. So, he wondered is finding the truth of God the purpose of man? Science measured things microscopically and measured nothing at all, which reminded him he remembered someone once say to become holy you must become nothing, but you can't tell you're holy because you are no thing. If God is no thing. He remembered the scripture when Jesus said, "I Am that I Am." What is that? The all and everything. Trevor remembered reading somewhere God cannot be thought.

Isn't the truth Trevor thought God is both macroscopic and microscopic. A word doesn't describe nature because you can say "tree" and everyone will have a different picture. Nature is over and above our labels and language. We can only understand nature in bits and pieces with various laws of science, which are part of natural law. Discoveries and inventions give us titles and names. Nature communicates too in vibes to man. Man's language is minimal and specific. The only way we can search for truth is with words, but the language of the soul cannot be comprehended.

Nature presents itself in patterns like moving water, electromagnetic waves or photons. Trevor was reading articles on quantum physics online. The waves in the sea were like electromagnetic waves or photon waves. This was seen as a partial truth. Physics helps us understand nature and the patterns nature uses to communicate. The language of nature is beyond science because of spirituality. He concluded earth and nature were alive. Truth is in spirituality, a thin line between that and science. Mankind was using science to move into higher realms of theology in his search for truth.

Trevor was interested in trying to figure out what was happening. The world was getting smarter about God. He felt as well this was only the tip of the iceberg and was trying to understand the helicoid. Seashells have a helicoid pattern as do human imprints, leaves, tornadoes, and other natural phenomena. He was digging into mathematical forms in nature. We are just using science to understand the truth. Theologians were pointing to the Pi, trigonometric and exponential series found in nature. This stuff was over his head. He was getting to a saturation point for knowledge and understanding. The man reaches higher when he goes beyond the objective point of view to abstract points of view. He kept reading on and understood man comes to a higher truth with mathematical laws, physical laws, equations and findings at the abstract concept level.

All these different religions in the world have what they say is the truth? What is the ultimate truth? A truth that embodies all of nature. What is that which governs nature and man in and out? He was back to God is invisible unless we are looking at God in nature. No one knew. Objectivity and science seem to be pointing back to religion. He read once where the theologians would ask the scientists when they got to the mountaintop, "what took you so long"?

He wanted to look into the helicoid and Fibonacci series more. The only thing he gathered was science starts at a point, eventually points to spirituality and infinity, which circles back in on itself. The center of the whole helicoid is connected. Objectivity and measurement are all part of the same thing. We are trying to polarize and box up. A philosopher remarked once we figure life out, "the only thing to do now is have a good laugh." Days passed since he checked in with Kiana. He saw her as spiritual and religious and wondered what she would have to say about all this. He would temper his approach to this wounded soul he knew well.

Chapter Fifteen: **A Heart Light As A Feather**

R uth tried to spend the day out with her autistic four-year-old girl Anne. Communication with her and tempering her emotions remained daily challenges. She stayed at home and her husband worked full time. He stayed home when he could. They came to the gardens on several occasions before to be out in nature and to relax. It, a place not about routine. Eli viewed all kinds of people who came to the botanical gardens every year. Being springtime, it started to heat up. People in South Florida didn't like the cold and the cooler temps started to evaporate leaning into spring. The little girl stayed close to mom and her mom, good at keeping an eye on her daughter. Everything here remained about nature because it stood not about thought, but more about observing and feeling. Being a mom of a four-year-old with autism, a lot of work. She took her daughter to applied behavioral analysis, play therapy and occupational therapy. They came here to get away from it all and all the efforts to make sure her development gelled as much as possible. Though nothing seemed to relax her daughter more than coming to the botanical gardens.

Eli recognized her every time. The little girl, not about thoughts and knowledge, but reflected presence and experience. A moderate crowd today. A waterfall at least twelve feet high stood out and it cascades down a rock face covered with lush plantings, adding the splash and gurgle of rushing water to the rainforest soundscape. It created a delicate mist than enhances the rainforest ambiance. The waterfall pool provides opportunities to educate visitors about the water cycle. A pool right next to the waterfall that held almost 30,000 gallons of water gushed. The waterfall remained a continuous stream and lulled people into a trance. A cool place to contemplate the majesty of the rainforest environment. Aquatic rainforest plants showed the relationship between water, plants, and ecosystems. It stood out as the most peaceful spot in the whole botanical gardens. In the late afternoon, the sun moved over the Gulf of Mexico. People milled around and enjoyed their surroundings. The woman and her daughter stared at the waterfall-like everyone else did. Ruth summoned Anne as if it became time to leave and turned to start walking away and looked back at her daughter who stared at the waterfall, but with a look of wonder and awe on her face. The little girl pointed and said, " a lady" with exuberance in her voice. Ruth didn't see anything and she looked hard to see anything. Other people looked at her daughter pointing and she became embarrassed. "Come on honey, let's go," she said. They drew attention and her daughter remained transfixed. She took Anne by the hand and looked a little bit longer because she loved her daughter and wanted to believe her.

Everyone noticed the silence and calm that over took the gardens. Ruth became worried and with so much on her mind and at times Anne would have complete meltdowns because she didn't have the words to say what she wanted. Ruth, afraid, thought that might happen here. She stood letting her daughter look at what she did not understand. Ruth wondered if her daughter became delusional or psychotic? No evidence of that appeared with anyone in her family or her husband's family to be psychotic.

They got to the car after about thirty minutes. Then mom started the inquisition, "a pretty lady" the daughter emphasized. Ruth remained beside herself, but her daughter, completely peaceful. Her parents, atheists and kept that pretty much a secret. "What lady"? the mom asked as they drove home. The little girl in the back of the SUV became frustrated because for her it could only be simple and her mom made it into a problem. Other children viewed the same thing the same day at different times. They all said the same thing to their parents. Parents became nervous about sharing this information with other parents.

Anne had very few words with which to describe what happened and Ruth became intrigued. They had to go to the grocery store on the way home and made their way in to get some things for dinner that night. Ruth didn't guess what to tell her husband. What the mom wasn't saying, a tremendous sense of peace came over her she as her daughter looked at the lady. The little girl wanted so her mom appeased her as they made their run through the store and got her donuts with sprinkles. They got into a checkout line where the magazines and candy bars could be found. The tabloids boasted stars and the latest news that surrounded their lives. Ruth, in a daze, waited for her place in line. Anne pointed again like she did at the gardens. A periodical that circulated as a reissue of a classic edition. On the cover, a title, Women of the Bible. "The lady" Anne kept her hand straight out and pointing." "the lady "? Ruth asked her. The little girl's answer, "yes."

Chapter Sixteen: **Did You Hear The News?**

The two sat together and shared the space by tragedy. "Did you hear about the little girl in Sarasota? Kiana asked. "No, I don't see the news much. What's in Sarasota besides a nice town and great beach?" Trevor asked. "A little girl who went to these gardens with her mom reported seeing a pretty lady. The mom made nothing of things other than being perplexed. She kept questioning her daughter thinking her to be delusional and she didn't want to say anything because she didn't understand how people would respond. That's not the only thing. The mom and daughter had been going to the gardens for quite a while as the daughter diagnosed with leukemia had been receiving treatments for some time. The mom would go to the garden as a respite from all the doctor's appointments and treatments to get outside. Well, one day they went and to a waterfall. Her little girl looked surprised and was pointing. Her mom asked her what she pointed at and she had said the pretty lady. The mom had to explain this to her husband that night. The next day they went in for treatment and had blood work done. The doctors and nurses noticed how healthy she looked all of a sudden. The next morning the doctor called the parents to speak to them. When they consulted with the doctor, he told them their daughter had no trace of leukemia. The parents became ecstatic. They couldn't stop talking. I read this on the news today. Other children told their parents a pretty lady smiled at them and now people are flocking to the gardens.

Kiana experienced the intensity of her grief and didn't want to reveal how much she wanted to believe and became excited about what she told Trevor. She had been studying different apparitions and realized people to be interested in Jesus and Mary outside the faith and church. Anything outside of those lines, met with a predictable and certain skepticism. She remained careful. Trevor, her son's best friend, not in that religious inner circle. She knew him to be a curious onlooker. With that in mind, she allowed herself a certain spontaneity. So much of life to her seemed intermingled with self-control and spontaneity. She thought of herself as being one of more self-control than anything. Religious, conforming, cautious and pious at times. With the death of her husband and now son, her self-control became an extreme.

For Kiana, God remained the epitome of self-control and spontaneity. The universe is ordered and God is running fine without any help from us. Creation and order are parts of the same life. Spontaneity called to her because one could be found to be more alive while letting go. With funerals, social norms, grieving processes and the like, life took her to numb. Part of getting older she realized, not caring what others thought. Apparitions, nothing new and seen in a skeptical manner. Regardless she looked to the most recent occurrence in the southwest part of Florida. The story touched her heart.

"Wow! I didn't hear of those things happening in the United States. Most of the time something like that happens in other parts of the world like Bosnia, Portugal, Rwanda and France. So, something like that is rare in this country" Trevor said with no judgment. He had a spectacular curiosity about God, religion, and spirituality. That door may be the one that allows people more than any other to sense we are divine or are God. Are we God or are we not God? Hinduism interested him along with native American shamanism. Consciousness and mindfulness seemed to him to be watered down words.

"God shows up in so many ways to so many people around the world and everybody lives in different paradigms they grow up in. Mine, always Catholicism, Jesus, and Mary. The holy family, a model on how to live. I believe they are all still alive" Kiana said reflecting on her faith. She added "so many people in the world are not Christians or Catholics. They come from different traditions with their beginnings and endings in the world. Sounds like a great place to get lost. I listened to a lecture once about the people who switch faiths to have the hardest time. Trees don't like to be uprooted most of the time. This is what I'm used to, but I don't judge someone because they came from another tradition. Jesus to me is part of the holy trinity, the triune God. In the beginning, the Word, that's what I believe, but I'm no judge so I will leave that up to God"

"I always wondered about that. How would God know someone is going to be Jewish their whole life or Hindu and never convert to Christianity and make them suffer eternal torment? I don't believe Jesus didn't die and rise from the dead. I'm wondering about all this other stuff like

Jewish mysticism, Buddhism, Hinduism, and all the other religions" Trevor responded.

"You would be wise to be careful spiritually I mean," said Kiana. She went on to talk about a topic that astounded her. " Many of which the church reported to be valid and many not. The most recent ones in Medjugorje the pope doesn't believe to be real because of the sheer frequency. All those people in the countryside praying and surrounding one of the visionaries and Mary appeared to the lady since her youth. The sightings are frequent as you can see on the internet. Everyone becomes silent and still because the lady looks up smiles and weeps at times during an apparition. The pope said he doesn't believe Our Lady shows up every day like she is delivering the mail. What would be this lady's gain by going through this every day with all those people? Is she delusional and creating this mass hysteria or stirring would be a better word among all these people? People travel from all over the world. Then, is the Zeitoun in the 1960s where she appeared to over 500,000 people, but she said nothing. So, the whole thing is baffling and mysterious. I read where Zeitoun means olive the place is where Joseph and Mary went when they fled to Egypt" Kiana added.

She went on "a story about a man who, a builder in the 1920s who wanted to build on the site and had a dream of the Virgin Mary who told him she would honor the place if a church would be built on the spot and became St. Mark's Coptic Church. You might think I'm crazy. Fascinating and yet the more people talk about these things the more people think that person is crazy or telling the truth. I believe we are skeptical, but things of God are not always made for the rational skeptical mind."

" I saw a story on the internet about that. Christians, Jews, Muslims, and atheists , all present. I believe with overt signs people will still be skeptical. I had this crazy idea that God is just God and is for the most part undefinable. God is so vast, tall, wide and deep, not everyone will maintain the same ideas about the subject. Different religions maintain their ideas about God. Like Einstein said religion and science are branches of the same tree. The way my brain works I think religions are like a sort of condiment. They each add a certain flavor like ketchup on a burger and mayonnaise on fries, which some people balk at," Trevor shared with a giggle. I think if we don't try to find God in all this we stir around in nothingness.

Through each one's grief, people searched for God and meaning all while under a heavy blanket of sorrow. "I wonder how they decide if an apparition is real or not. I wonder if the apparition could be real if the church says no" inquired Trevor. "Conyers Georgia is another one not validated. People are easy to be deceived because people do want to believe", Kiana said.

"We should go as like an apparition scavenger hunt. Not to disrespect, but to investigate the phenomenon. That story about the lady whose little daughter healed of leukemia came out that the lady didn't believe in God is nothing short of amazing" Trevor said with an elevated inflection in his voice.

"Yes," said Kiana "reports say other children were telling their parents the same thing that they had seen a lady. She didn't report saying anything to the children. A buzz in the community surfaced. I don't think the people who run those botanical gardens right next to the ocean want all that attention. Rumors of spontaneous healings were occurring and this is generating a lot of attention. Seems fascinating and a nice place to visit even if nothing was happening, she said."

Trevor punctuated the moment and said "Here we are. We both miss Tracy. We're both continuing to search spiritually and in different ways. You've been a Catholic your whole life and I am an unspecified spiritual seeker who won't align with any religion, which doesn't mean I don't believe in God. We're pretty different, but Tracy was the one thing we had in common. I think I am naturally curious and would like to know or learn as much as I can. You are a woman of faith and someone with a lot more faith than me. We both read about this story at the same time. I think you're interested because of your faith and devotion. I'm interested in something that sounds miraculous at the same time and true."

Kiana responded, "It comes down to faith. I have friends who have been to Lourdes in France. I read about Our Lady of Kibeho in Rwanda. She revealed herself as the Mother of the Word. Fascinating. She warned the people about the coming genocides long before they occurred. She was trying to help. It wouldn't have happened if the country turned to God. If I heard she was appearing there in Florida, I would go." "I would go. We can go. Sounds crazy" said Trevor. They both looked at each other and smiled.

Kiana went on "part of me feels a little foolish I must admit kind of like a spiritual ambulance chaser and part of that is a spark of curiosity filled with a childlike wonder. I don't care what other people think. In my life, I've been through so much I'm aware the part of me that cared a little too much about what other people think and can accept in myself that part that is fascinated by the Immaculate Conception. I don't at the same time get caught up and waste time on something that is just foolish."

"That's funny you should say that," Trevor said. "I read in one of the books I have been reading that self- acceptance is the psychological and spiritual equivalent of space. Which is meant to say that in space you have the sun, the moon, the stars the galaxies and everything else. So, the more accepting we are of ourselves, the more the possibilities open up for things to happen. What's with all these apparitions? I find the topic fascinating like the Jews had the ark that had the ten commandments, the staff of Moses and a pot of manna. Astounding stuff. I heard that Mary is the ark of the new covenant because she carried Jesus the Redeemer who is God the Son of the Trinity. If the ark of the covenant had the ten commandments, considered very powerful and holy, how much more Mary who carried the son of God. That religious storytelling is what makes God so interesting to me because of this mixture of truth, power, holiness and just fascinating stories. "

"It's so easy I know and even for myself to get caught up in this hysteria that can put you in a religious nut category and like sheep we follow so that is part of the reason I have Jesus so that I can follow him. We need a light to follow. My mother told me once in my life before she died that if you have Jesus and Mary on your side, you can't lose. When she told me this, she had a lightness in her voice and a smile. The beauty and simplicity of her faith were remarkable," Kiana added.

"You're a lot like that. Trevor went on to say, "You are such a solid person who went through so much and handled everything with immense grace. I don't know how you do it." For a moment Kiana's thoughts were of Mary and how much she endured watching her son being tormented was a torment for her and how it must have been a torment for Jesus to have his mother watch him be tortured. She thought Mary was so docile and endured so much. The whole time she was saying yes to God and she lowered herself more than ever to the will of the Father and became raised to a unique and holy level. This is what she believed in her heart. Mary was a mother she could now identify herself with and was close to her in the most important and yet spiritual way in her own heart and soul. Thoughts and ideas were only ways that pointed to her whom she now knew to be her mother more than ever. It was a personal knowing in her soul that was indescribable. Words to her were ornamental only. There is a part of life that words don't describe like trying to describe nature. She felt the same about God. The experience is beyond words.

Kiana was like a mom to Trevor. Trevor's parents divorced when he was little and he spent his youth bouncing back and forth like a ship between two islands that always had a little too much emotional cargo. This left him feeling a little less secure and his search for God in religion was him trying to find security in the world. Religion and its search for him were trying to connect on a deeper level with his parents. He felt a sense of God to be an indescribable near yet far off parent who loved him whom he sought a deeper connection with. Kiana, on the other hand, had a solid foundation from the beginning and yet her life was the opposite of Trevor's to a degree in that her family or foundation in the human world was being stripped away from her while Trevor was trying to build what remained of his. And so, they sought common ground.

Chapter Seventeen: You're Reading About What?

Ron got back home to Tampa. Wretched in his heart, the fact that he got to his brother's bedside to say goodbye. This became one of those times he wanted to know why God did what he did. A bigger part of him wondered why God let him go through the things he went through. Most of his life he thought things happened to him. He now became bitter after his divorce. The divorce hurt his relationship with his kids and he bore the fissure in his heart. The lady in the hospital stood behind him from at a distance, but he couldn't remove her out of his mind. More so, she kept popping up in his mind.

They didn't even talk. Back to the moment, he started to unpack his suitcase. Even now she stood behind him in his mind. She could only be nothing more than a mystery. He couldn't understand why she made such a firm impression on his soul even. Alone, the accumulation of days since he found out that Quinn endured an accident, piled upon him. The tears came like a soft rain that no one hears. A bitter end is how life went for him much of the time. The way he and his brother were raised, his divorce, the end of another family and now this.

Ron held the book in his hand, the only thing of Quinn's that he possessed except his effects from the hospital room. The book, the oddest of all things. The questions stirred in him. Is this about God? Quinn, a religious nut? Jesus freak? The book told about sightings of the Virgin Mary in Portugal. This triggered his memory of going to mass at the Catholic church when he lived in foster care two times. He liked church because of the ceremony and because of the structure. The order of the mass made him know safe for some reason. Perhaps because church seemed to be about something much bigger than himself and what he went through. The idea of a holy family comforted him even though he never became Catholic.

Ron liked going to church when they lived in foster care as kids. Quinn always seemed restless and fought with the foster parents to let him go to the car early. Ron remained more compliant and enjoyed the mass. He liked the stories of the bible and the characters therein. The stories of the bible afforded him an escape from his everyday life of trying to get used to a new family. Sometimes he wished he could stay at the church when time to leave. He held mixed feelings about going to the teen group on Wednesday nights. He didn't want the other kids to know what he went through and always wanted to belong. A lot of cute girls showed up and he managed to establish a crush on one with blue eyes and blond hair. He didn't think she ever noticed him and remained interested, but not Quinn. What did Quinn do with this book?

Ron's mind did summersaults. Maybe Quinn found God at the end of his life and then died. Something inside made him feel good that his brother owned this book and that maybe he found something that made him happy. Each brother wanted the other brother to be happy. They always pulled for each other to have a win. Maybe this book helped Quinn get closer to God somehow. They kept in touch though not frequently.

Ron didn't go to church with his ex-wife but a handful of times and they never established themselves in any church. He held an affinity for the Catholic faith that he did not share. Because of the way his life went, he kept things to himself. The yearning to belong still remained in him. He and his wife would drink sometimes, but after they married, it got bad after a couple of years. He couldn't take it after she went so far. She acted as if it never happened with all the times she would pass out. After they divorced, he read a lot about addiction and the light came on for him. Many dynamics from his family background and from his marriage tied in together. Overtime through his voracious reading he began to understand himself and his life. He loved learning even though he didn't like school. A chaotic home life became the recipe for poor academic performance.

Ron got an inspiration to carry the flame that in his mind drove Quinn to connect with God. The back cover of the book referred to evangelization like the world has never seen. The book explores physical and spiritual questions and looks at it from all angles. Chronically bummed, he thought this book might pull him out of the doldrums. It returned him to the feeling of belonging to life.

The next day Ron did something he been wanted to do for a long time. People that he ran into on his job over time told him overtime to go to the grotto. He, silently remained a covert fan of the faith from afar. It's like people kept telling him to read The Shack. After two or three years he finally loved it. The same thing happened with the grotto in Tampa. People told him about it and the peace there. His interest stayed in the back of his mind as the lady in the hospital. She kept appearing in his memory. There must be something about her he thought to himself.

He drove to the Our Lady of Lourdes Grotto with apprehension the next day. The area looked beautiful and lush. It stood near some soccer fields and a small local university. He got out of his car and his serotonin got a boost. As he approached the grotto, a stillness permeated the air. He kept going and went right up to the statue of Mary with a child statue kneeling in supplication before her. This stood off to the center of the grotto where there remained an altar with several different flower pots. The flowers were real and there stood stands in the back of the grotto for candles if someone wanted to light or place one there. Plaques on either side of the grotto accented the location. Many candles flickered in front of the gold cross against the wall behind the altar. Candles displayed Jesus and Mary on them. Beautiful rolling hills went on forever on this perfect day. He decided to sit and pray as he called her The Immaculate Conception.

For a long time, he emptied and discussed everything in his spirit. His whole life up to now, their upbringing, being mad at God for letting him go through this and still going through this, his brother's death, the person that died from the car wreck and their family, his divorce and everything he could think of that made him suffer. He wanted to read the book that Quinn read. A grotto gift shop of all things stood nearby. Curiosity about what a grotto gift shop would have propelled him. People scattered around the area and as he walked toward the entrance of the store a lady came walking up to go into the store barely able to move her legs and moved slowly with her walker. She smiled at him very pleasantly as he held the door for her.

Ron went inside and observing the crosses, books, prints, rosaries and all sorts of items for personal effects or one's home. He browsed around and then he stopped in his tracks and recognized the man. Father Foley from St. Theresa's church from his childhood appeared in front of him. Father Foley looked at Ron and didn't recognize him,. between seventy-five and eighty years old with a gentle smile. "Hi, Father. Oh my God, I remember you from my childhood" Ron said. He went on, "Are you shopping here too"? Ron introduced himself and Father Foley remembered him astonishingly and who told Ron he also liked to shop here and that he volunteered at different churches in the area. Ron, mystified, carried on the conversation, but the irony and coincidence, mind-blowing.

Chapter Eighteen: **What's The Commotion?**

The botanical gardens attracted a lot of attention on an annual basis as a beautiful and peaceful place to visit. The little girl who survived leukemia, not the only one who witnessed a beautiful lady. Every parent remained mystified that their children told them what they did when at the gardens. The parents afraid to talk to anyone, did anyway. A buzz surrounded these events and many parents talked. Its prevalence elevating, but not without an equal amount of doubt. Each set of parents thought their child became unstable. Should they to take their child to their pediatrician or a therapist? Many people were aware of the healing and the child's mother's life turned right side up. At war with herself to believe when her whole life she didn't.

People tended to reject Marian apparitions and assume that those people who witness such things are just not stable. At the moment the whole scene presented itself outside of the box of the common everyday experiences of going to work, school, watching the news, attending sporting events, going to the beach and all the other things that people do in their everyday lives.

Kiana caught wind of the event on Catholic television. She read about the many apparitions that occurred all over the world. Only so many were sanctioned by the church as being real. Since the 1980s the Catholic Church peaked from afar at apparitions reported in Medjugorje. Though the church did not sanction the apparitions, they are now approving pilgrimages to the site and changing their position. She would love to go and learned the story about a little girl being healed of leukemia. This little girl visited the botanical gardens with her mom, an atheist. The mom refused to give out her name because she didn't want any more attention. The mom, a rigid atheist recognized that the miracle happened.

Some people who visited the botanical gardens mentioned that they thought that anyone who thought they witnessed something must be unstable. Some people interviewed on the local news thought the whole thing to be pure stupidity. One person reported that these were just a bunch of gullible Christians who needed to buy into something and got caught up in a mass delusion.

No one explained however what went on with all the kids. Many more skeptics existed than believers. The board of trustees, the advisory committee and the staff ran around trying to make things go according to plan. Family Saturdays, campaigns for the gardens and programs for family and schools attracted many. The gardens had lecture series, exhibits and remained a world-class center for education, research, and conservation. Weddings, classes, and tours occurred regularly. However, an excessive amount of murmuring began to disrupt the natural flow of things. People showed up to catch a glimpse of some happening supernatural. What looked like a significant increase in the amount of foot traffic, vaguely disguised onlookers trying not to be noticed. Parents didn't try to stand out and remained cautious not to be the one who said their kid had seen someone from heaven show up.

Human deception became widely discussed to explain the things that went on. The most uniform response, rejection. The dilemma beset the parents. If they say their kids witnessed The Virgin Mary then they risk being seen as fools or nuts. After rigorous investigation of reported apparitions such as in Fatima or Lourdes, the Catholic Church approved of the apparitions.

Trevor dug into the whole ordeal on his own. He and Kiana somewhat agreed that they would investigate. Kiana, more the believer and Trevor, the one with pure curiosity. To him, God dabbled in our world more than usual. People would say you would have to be out of your mind to believe this.

Trevor read reports online that evangelicals reported a plot to be a distraction to get our minds off of God and on to Mary. Evangelicals would say that Catholics don't want us to know the bible, but just to go along with that doctrine of Mary and worship her. In contrast, the Catholics would say that if you are close to Mary you will be closer than ever to Jesus. One thing for sure, the flames of talking about God certainly got fueled.

Trevor and Kiana were investigated whether they wanted to venture to South Florida. They looked for credible reasons to go. Baptized paganism became what the Evangelicals said the Catholic church did to get money out of people. Some people wanted to believe and there would be a duel with people who didn't want to believe and tried to debunk the whole thing. Everyone placed somewhere in between if not at either end. As far as Trevor understood, the possibility that the Blessed Virgin ever appeared to anyone would be rare.

Kiana focused on Our Lady of Fatima. She had a book on Marian apparitions. All the ones sanctioned by the church that is and stayed cozy spot in her home in her favorite church. Her little shrine set in front of her. A crown of thorns that came from a bush indigenous to Israel, a scapular representing her devotion to the Christian life, several rosaries, a candle, an image of Jesus on the cross that looked like an actual photograph, a photograph of her husband and now a picture of Tracy all before her.

In 1917, 70,000 people showed up at Fatima. All of the accounts she read had something wonderous about them. The sun did all sorts of miraculous things like radiate heat, came close and moved farther away, got bigger and smaller, changed colors and rotated like a wheel. A physician, an eye specialist viewed the sun surrounded by a scarlet flame, then yellow and purple. The sun seemed to be moving exceedingly fast and whirled. Three children said they had seen the Blessed Virgin Mother and they said she called herself The Lady of the Rosary who said she would perform a miracle and that many would have their faith strengthened and affirmed.

Trevor and Kiana looked up information on apparitions in their own homes from two different perspectives. Trevor read how hardened skeptics became convinced of what happened. He read that the first recorded appearance to be in 40 AD to the apostle James in Saragossa, Spain and that nearly 400 reported worldwide in the twentieth century. Trevor just tried to figure out apparitions. Visions are perceived internally while an apparition is perceived as an exterior event with sounds and smells. He found that apparitions are not interior voices, a trance or channeling because these have no external component. Kiana believed so she didn't need to know the mechanics.

Trevor learned that the biggest apparition ever took place from 1968 to 1971 in Cairo, Egypt. Appeared a luminescent image witnessed at the church of St. Mary in a part of Cairo. He looked the odd name up meaning olive in Arabic. Hundreds of thousands of people viewed the apparition and filmed it. The irony is that it is not well known. It is not a cultural or even a specific phenomenon. Some people say that sightings of extraterrestrials are apparitions. The whole notion of an apparition is that it carries a religious or spiritual message.

The Marian apparitions Trevor read are named after the towns they occurred in. Many different people have witnessed apparitions over time and large groups don't see apparitions more than small groups. Most often The Blessed Virgin appeared to young children and poor people. Trevor thought about the stories he heard about many children seeing The Virgin Mary sounds like many apparitions in the past.

Kiana focused on the apparitions. People throughout history have reported having seen The Virgin Mary whether they be saints or not. She read about the miracle of the sun at Fatima and understood however that God had his way of doing things and worked outside the laws of natural science because those laws don't apply to God. Sacrifice, penance, and reparation, the key messages of that apparition. Adoration, hope, and love encouraged the people along with constant prayer. She kept studying and learned that these apparitions were given as private messages and for many people.

Kiana wondered what the criteria would be for even evaluating the apparitions. She read where the person had to be practicing the faith, be obedient to the church, be moral, mentally balanced and honest. The report needed to be flawless and by a person who is not seeking financial gain or who is immoral. Cases are left open can endure time even for a century. She felt shocked that only 12 fell into the accepted category while 300 reports remained open. She became aware that she would be dead and gone by the time the church acknowledged that what had happened in Florida. For now, only rumors. Sometimes a local bishop or church may approve of an apparition. The Roman Catholic Church doesn't approve of apparitions just because a local official or church approves.

She felt confused because she had just saw a video of a neurosurgeon talk about an extensive and elaborate near-death experience, he had wherein he reported no hell existed. In one of the secrets, this could be avoided by devotion to The Immaculate Heart of Mary.

Mary told the children about a great light in the sky about the start of the second great war. The secrets and apparitions revealed during the time of the Russian revolution when many people turned away from the faith. To Kiana that Mary warned people like a mother warns her children to watch out. She thought everyone can understand that. Kiana remembered from one of her books that Mary said she is the mother of all living beings on earth. Apparitions come at times when sin permeates mankind when plummeting into darkness. Kiana thought that Mary tried to help us prevent disaster by encouraging people to turn to God.

Kiana thought even with more evidence of something holy occurring in Florida that most people just wouldn't believe. She wanted to get excited about after all the heartache she had been through and understood in her soul that knowing that Mary had shown up in her lifetime would help to give her so much hope and faith. Kiana wouldn't stop believing in God.

On the other hand, she had been aware that the apparitions caused the conversion of millions of people to Roman Catholicism. She read where millions of people went to apparition sites each year. Her favorite apparition, Our Lady of Guadalupe who appeared to Juan Diego. The story of how the Archbishop did not believe and then later became convinced to the point that the archbishop ordered a shrine be built in her honor.

The details of the whole story are remarkable, especially the part of where she spoke to Juan Diego and how the cloth said to be part of that apparition showed no signs of deterioration. She remembered her trip to Mexico City with her late husband and Tracy and knows 8 million people became Catholic faith between 1532 and 1538.

Who can make sense of a real apparition and just basic mass delusion? She had articles on her desk about scientists who have done extensive research on the sensed presence and how the brain can generate this. A scientist suggested one of the mass sightings be based upon geophysical fluctuations. Science collided with her faith.

Chapter Nineteen: **Science for New Believer**

T revor went out on his own. He remembered when Tracy and he got a place together and he teased Tracy about staying at home for so long, but he couldn't blame him because Tracy's mom, like a mom to him as well. When his parents split up in grade school, he spent most of his time going back and forth between their homes and so he became more familiar with a broken home than a meshed one. He became friends with Tracy and they often hung out together at Tracy's where Trevor liked to go. The family used to live in Hawaii and moved to Texas where Tracy's dad retired. That home, more like home to him than anything. He has seen Kiana lose her husband Tom and now his best friend and brother as much as anything.

Trevor, aware of the pain that Kiana went through, helpless to do anything. The heaviness lumbered like a dense cloud. The only light in Kiana, when they talked about apparitions and how she talked about her faith ever since he went over to their house the first time. On the wall of her home, pictures of Jesus or Mary, Kiana lived her life because of them. Invisible and visible at the same time.

He explored over the last few years Buddhism, Judaism, Christianity, The Tao, Hinduism and now he came upon the apparitions through talking with Kiana over time. Over time she would weave that topic into the conversation at their house. She spoke about them like talking about a trip to Disney and she always wanted to go and never went. He loved her like a mom and wanted to help her to find happiness. She briefly mentioned that the stirring in Florida about a child seeing a lady at a botanical gardens. To him, at first, the stirring seemed like an outlandish and absurd idea.

The Virgin Mary didn't interest him as much as what happened. Trevor knew that God had no limits so why couldn't this happen? He knew people to be easily swept up into funnel clouds of religion he called them that often ended up hurting people especially in the case of people who followed a preacher with ill intent. Spiritually or religiously speaking,

Trevor became more of a renegade than anything else. He enjoyed scouting out the divine landscape and grew up in the arena of Christianity and he liked to move around vantage points in the arena. A particularly interesting seat to him. He heard the angles about Mary and of people taking issue with her as just another woman who happened to give birth to Jesus. Part of his reading tour took him to Christian mysticism wherein he read that Mary's parents took her to the temple at a young age and she stayed practicing her faith in her early years praying for the Messiah to come. She, selected by God say from the beginning of time to be the Mother of Christ. It seemed to him that people viewed her as nothing more than common, some revered her and believed she to be the Immaculate Conception based upon of course their particular upbringing. He remembered in the book about her apparitions in Medjugorje that reported her to say "come close to my Immaculate Heart and you will discover God." Someone he talked to once told him that you can be close to Jesus, but if you are close to Mary, you will be closer to Jesus than ever. She became like the mom always warning her children about the dangers to avoid that moms typically do. Except she did this for mankind.

Trevor remembered how many times he dismissed his mother. He reproached himself for not making the effort to do so. She tried to support him and work like crazy. He and his dad started to become even closer over the years. He, an only child and became independent early in his life. His friendship with Tracy and his family started early and sparked his interest in God because the closeness in the family he longed for seemed to appear in a family close to God. Drawn in and independent at the same time.

An element of mystery surrounded the apparitions and Trevor dug around. He, more like an archeologist than a believer and couldn't prove it not to be a grand deception. He recalled reading somewhere in the bible that even the very elect were capable of being deceived. People write books sharing personal powerful accounts that seemed powerful, inspiring and beautiful. A human being can perceive different kinds of energy and not know how to explain most of it. People are electromagnetic conductors of energy just like a pool skimmer. If the lightning struck the pool skimmer while a person is holding it, they get struck.

Trevor wondered if apparitions were scientific. He looked up the apparitions at Medjugorje. It turned out that people studied different aspects of the apparitions extensively. Scientists studied the eyes, hearing, breathing, skin conductivity and cortical functioning of the visionaries. Six people started having visions of her in their childhood. They report that the visions occurred for 38 years. Trevor found this very hard to believe and remembered recently seeing a story that the Pope said that the Mother of God doesn't show up as a postman every day. The church did not approve this apparition. Hundreds of thousands if not millions of people flocked to the area. Many believed and converted to Catholicism in scores.

Whoever, the scientists concurred that these people indeed shared something of an ecstatic state. Synchronicity of the experiences are what stood out to him. The visionaries bowed their heads, kneeled, verbally responded at the same time. This apparition, not experienced by the normal pathways in the brain, seemed to be anesthetized.

No one proved that any of the visionaries to be epileptic, mentally ill or hysterical. Everyone who is looking into the mystery is trying to figure out the source of the apparitions including the Vatican. Trevor realized that six people viewed the same thing on repeated occasions and they appear to be stable people. This became a treasure chest for him as he read that some wondered if this happened in India would people worship Shiva. His mind quickly took him back to Zeitoun and how Mary appeared where Islam is the state religion. The Coptic church has a large church. No verbal message during those apparitions occurred. Then he remembered reading up on Medjugorje where Mary reportedly said that she is the mother of all living beings on earth. What a joy it would be for Kiana to go and see Mary. One could look at that like it to be the craziest thing one could do in their lives because most people take trips or vacations to do everything else. He noted there to be constant regular pilgrimages to the sites where apparitions took place like Lourdes and Medjugorje.

What is it about this place where this child saw this lady? Why this little girl? People started to gather at the botanical gardens where the siting took place. It could not be the kind of attention they expected there and those in charge remained in a quandary about whether to shoo away those gathered and praying. Trevor watched the news to see if anything else happened at the location. The main sources of the news did not reporting anything. Because of technology and the internet, the news became national or global. People became inundated with news every day so much so that unlike the old days. The observer to choose what story they wanted to read about and watch whenever they wanted.

The personal experience that each person shared never reflected anything having to do with ego. Nearly frenetic about the event in Florida, he tried to figure out why this phenomenon occurred in the first place. The scientists in the studies he brushed up on indicated that there to be one part of the brain that perceived the apparition and other parts that didn't. Still, the question had no answer as to the origin of the apparition itself. Can we connect to another level of reality if heaven allows it? There seems to be an unexplained ability of humans to tap into a source that is beyond scientific explanation. Trevor thought that those in whatever power could use the apparitions to manipulate people for their gain. He thought it would be good to be careful to not wholeheartedly dive in and believe the events without investigation. So many people faced a wide barrage of responses if they went to go to an apparition site. Something within him opened him up to the possibility.

Chapter Twenty: **Mystified**

Weary and beginning to drift away from sedatives and exhaustion, she never believed in God or any higher power. Most of the time she did not have any energy anyway. Very often she grieved her daughter's illness making it difficult for her to get along with anyone. Hopelessness about the future had been the norm for her. Did she do something for God to punish her? It remained very difficult for her to pay attention. She only could be productive when trying to keep her daughter alive and keeping leukemia from killing her daughter. She avoided a normal life by going to doctors' appointments and enduring the uncertainty of treatments and would just die herself if the disease claimed her daughter. On good terms with herself, foreign. The only escape, sleep.

The sky became black except for a tiny opening above her head to the left where she viewed a small portion of white clouds and blue sky. The boat rocked from the side to side. Her arms gripped the tiny little boat she rode in. The waves turned into walls all around her and the boat pitched down and up steeply as it took all of her strength to hold on and her grip waned. Terrified and nothing else to do she hung on, the only thing keeping her alive. Waves crashed into other waves turning the sea into cresting white caps and she had no idea what direction she headed into. Off in the distance, she looked at another boat bigger than hers and with a sail. It too did the same thing reckless and out of control and looked at any moment that it might turn over and her eyes locked in on the vessel that did no better than her own. At brief moments she would lose visual contact and fall deeper into despair and hopelessness. The boat would reappear doing the same thing in a different location. She wondered if they saw her. They did the same thing by trying to control the boat frantically without succumbing to the sea. She got closer every time they disappeared and reappeared. The boat, filled with men who worked desperately to save themselves. The storm had pushed the boats closer and she thought they would crash into each other. What if they all die at sea? Her mind panicked and both boats were swamped by the waves and headed closer and closer towards each other.

The men on the boats dressed like people from another time frantic and she stared at a man in the stern. He slept and the men tried to wake him up as she wondered if their boats would collide. The man got up and she heard him yell "Peace! Be Still." The wind ceased and with a great calm. She got closer to their boat. Filled with awe she viewed that the man looked at her and said, "Ruth, why are you so afraid? Have you still no faith?" Eternity in his eyes. "Jesus," she said with the greatest joy and relief. Waking to the daylight immediately her daughter Anne came to her in the bed with such a serene look on her face not knowing the tremendous relief her mom felt at that moment after the visitation.

Chapter Twenty One: **The Dancing Sun**

R on dove into the book not fancy and short by nature. He opened the book before and read a line or two at most. The story would tell him that scores of people showed up that October 13th day in 1917. A prophecy told to the kids to whom Our Lady of Fatima appeared indicated a miracle on that day. At the same time even with countless witnesses, he found that his mind just blocked any possibility of truth. Ron lived his whole life in a world to him where miracles occurred very far and few between. He remained baffled as to why his brother would be reading about such a thing and especially about the Virgin Mary. Ron didn't think that Quinn searched for God. Quinn's life all too well, a storm that appeared inescapable. Ron hoped that his brother at least got to an island at the end.

He opened the book not so much to force himself to believe the miracle, but more so to become closer to his brother and dove into the ocean of words and saw things like never before. Ron didn't try to be brilliant and figure out God. To him, God remained something beyond human reasoning. He remained willing to allow immensity of the miracle to affect him and remembered that Einstein commented that the two predominant ways to look at life, that everything is or is not a miracle. He sat on the beach in Clearwater very late in the afternoon when the sun went from hot to warm, the middle of July. The wind at the ocean pushed back the humidity. The sound of the waves lapping on the shore, the sky with its clouds in the far distance announcing an approaching thunderstorm to him, divine art at every moment.

Ron would sit and read and then lookup. The story tried to compete with the sky and the beach. People traced across the beach in both directions. Today, just the right amount of people. Seagulls flew overhead while Pelicans dived into the ocean. Nature in all its warmth and power. With so much to let go of, life remained ever challenging. Now with his brother gone and this book in his hand. He read again and then some. The dancing of the sun to be compared to God parting the Red Sea for the entire Jewish nation? Why would Quinn read about this? Marian apparitions occurred in Medjugorje. Yet the Catholic Church does not approve of those apparitions. Since the church has not officially approved of these apparitions, many don't believe. The evidence however to Ron became overwhelming. Scores of videos of crowds at Medjugorje. His parents, fanatics of another variety so anything in the extreme induced caution in him. He didn't want to be anyone's fool when involving his spirit.

In Fatima, the appearance of the Virgin Mary to a few children and in Medjugorje, four people whom Mary consistently appear to impressed him. In Florida, one little girl reported to her mom whom she had seen at the botanical gardens. Mary begins appearing to children. Ron thought she did this because children to be pure, innocent and uncorrupted by the world. Was Mary warning the world of impending doom if the world didn't turn towards God? The opinion in his mind, that the country stood closer to God when and before he grew up. Then life seemed more wholesome and not complicated and fast like today's world with technology. The technological advances took over making life easier for people in general. People also gravitated away from nature. We use our phones to connect to others instead of physically moving somehow to do so like walking, biking or driving in a car even. Life became easier for us more so many things had become almost effortless.

We are more capable of connecting than ever before. Part of him believed as many people believed that all the technology that created a diversion or distraction from our spiritual life. Ron didn't want to embark on that research. Mary would only ever be just Jesus' mom and that's an opinion or argument that he didn't want to step into either. With all the apparitions that have occurred and all the people attending them, even good people were not immune from being deceived and the part of the bible about false signs and prophecies came to mind. Something happened sixty miles south of where he lived now. Supernatural and Divine, he would have to make up his mind.

The constant ocean breeze, a warm blanket constantly flowing and keeping him warm at the same time. Seagulls on occasion flew in search of food. He remembered throwing bread and chips to them as a child on the rare occasion when he went to the beach. By the time the church approved of any apparition in South Florida he figured he would be long gone. Only sixty miles away. So close. Mary is our spiritual mother and the author stressed the importance of growing up in a home with a spiritual mother and family. Ron didn't have anything like that growing up. He remembered anarchy. Quinn looked at the church to be just another person not to trust. Quinn would make arguments that people in churches hurt people too. Not as defended as his brother, Ron understood why his brother thought the way he did. What was going on in galaxies far away? In this galaxy he concluded, the mother of Jesus showed up to countless numbers of people.

The moon in the sky that afternoon looked like a little bit had been shaved off the bottom. He loved this part of the day, very warm and not sizzling hot, like earlier in the day. The most peaceful, at the beach. When younger, he would come here getting away from his parents. What a great contrast between his chaotic predictable home to the parameters of the ocean, beach, and sky. There remained nothing in front of him except for the ocean and sky that went on forever. In reality, he faced due west and straight across the Gulf of Mexico stood Texas. The book posed the idea that just as it would be important to have a spiritual father, why would it not be just as important to have a spiritual mother? The hope of connecting to his earthly father and mother, constantly shattered.

Most of the times he had talked about God with people with his inquisitiveness. Deep inside of him, a seed of faith grew. He found them to be indifferent, dismissive or neutral. When it came to people in the heavens, they didn't know what to do with this kind of information. People remained skeptical, not a bad thing to him. Come to think of it he just remembered that someone the other day had said "don't worry about what other people think of you, they are not thinking of you at all." We are raised in an atmosphere as children in a system of rewards and consequences and are conditioned to think of what other people think of us. The more dreadful the experience, the more we would be conditioned to seek the approval of the other rather than being affirmed as we are and don't know we are taking on peoples' poison.

Ron was drawn into it all despite all of his analyses about Fatima, Medjugorje, and people in general. One aspect that solidified it all for him remained that Mary became animated by the Holy Spirit for our benefit, the spouse of the Holy Spirit. He had only been to the gardens once even though he lived a little more than an hour away. Part of him thought that it to be absurd and psychotic that Jesus' mom showed up just down the road. A holy and divine creature showing up nearby on local soil, too much to completely put his head around.

The holy family appealed to him on the occasions when he went to a Catholic Church. It had been enough for him to be at peace. Routines or traditions provided a semblance of order. It seemed people easily believed that Catholics worshipped Mary. He understood it as she always pointed to Jesus and not herself. God allowed her the grace to call out to her children to warn them, to be beside them and protect them from spiritual and physical danger. Ron always intuitively knew her to be so powerful on that day he saw the image of Our Lady of Sorrows. Miracles hadn't occurred on-demand as such the way the world is today with comforts, luxuries, and convenience galore. Thoughts about what Jesus referred to a wicked generation asks for a sign. Jesus performed miracles for skeptics. Could the miracle of the sun be for skeptics? Could the same be said for Mary? Ron read once where Jesus told a mystic that He operates outside of the physical laws of nature. Scientists could study apparitions and miracles. The Einstein quote about everything being a miracle and nothing being a miracle came up in his mind like a hiccup. These two ways of looking at life varied widely among people. She conveyed messages of her Son during times of trials and tribulations like a mom telling her kids to watch out.

The lightning kept appearing in a new pattern every time. One would go straight down to the water and one off to the left as far as his eye could see. Ron knew many of the educated would try to analyze and intellectualize the apparitions. Restlessness made it hard for him to just sit on the beach and read with all the distractions surrounding him. A little plane flew overhead towing a banner and an airliner approached the Tampa airport. When people had to be right and proud, they focused on materialism and achievement, less inclined to God's word. To Ron, America became more materialistic and less spiritually strong than it used to be. Too many worldly activities to be attracted to the cross. He would be with this book awhile. His mind remained distracted. It became all too much to soak in and not to be devoured. Like a little cloud by itself, his conscience waited for it to turn into a bigger system. Tiny clouds don't get much attention though a big weather system does. He wondered if it would become anything at all. Could all this be the need for renewed spirituality? Once in a taxi when he left the airport on his flight back, the driver when talking about the volcanic eruptions in Hawaii, mother nature is divine energy. When a man turns against God, mother nature turns against man. Did it all go that deep? Is the earth a living thing connected to us and God? Do we invite destruction by turning away from our Creator? Did Mary tell us we have gone too far from home.

The last thing he wanted to do, to get into church doctrine because that killed any joy in it for him. To put Mary in a shell or one's faith and to say it is exactly this is a thing to him that becomes lifeless. The knock-on Catholicism, he understood as worshiping of saints. Could Mary be the biggest lighthouse ever pointing to God? In essence, he thought so because she delivered Eternal Light! In the back of his mind, he has been paying attention to the news of apparitions since young adulthood like something on the back wall of his awareness. He had thought that the sun had only danced at Fatima. The sun had danced, had become a void, spun, danced, pulsated, danced back and forth in a various array of colors. It fell into the realm of strange stories and amazing facts.

Ron assumed that his brother raced for the finish line to God before he died. For him, the little girl did see a beautiful lady, the mother of Jesus. That would be the best thing in his life. If it happened it wouldn't take him long to get there. He hoped like a little kid excited to see a favorite relative coming to town. A note of anticipation elevated in his soul. He had been duped countless times before by his mom. At some point, he had decided that life could not be trusted. Mistrust, doubt, guilt, confusion, feelings that challenged him like a swarm of negativity from his upbringing. For once in his life, he realized he needed something deep down to be in sync with. Silently he held out the hand of his spirit waiting for someone to reach back.

Chapter Twenty-Two: **Again?**

The local diocese in southwest Florida got wind of what happened at the botanical gardens. Father Francis at the local Catholic church became swarmed with calls and people coming up to him after mass asking about what the little girl saw. It's not that he didn't want to believe, in his sixties and worn out and ready to retire. At the end of the day, he loved to go home and relax with a scotch. In his conscience the Holy Ghost nudged him to go the botanical gardens before.

Ruth lived in a different paradigm. Here she stood only days ago not having any faith. To her, religion seemed to be folklore and the local creation story indigenous to the area. She understood that different religions maintained their creation myths. Her passion, to study epistemology. The whole study of belief and opinion fascinated her. She, a stay home mom, took care of a very sick little girl until days ago. Ruth didn't even pray for Anne's healing. Her first reaction, to find a way to not believe. The news of her daughter's experience spread from the doctor's office into the community like fig ivy. Ivy doesn't look like it is growing. The word spread slowly person to person. She went back at the Gardens again this time with Anne and her husband Paul. Her daily routine of excessive worry and preoccupation, replaced with calm and relief. Anne, the one least affected by it all. Now in the late afternoon, they stood right next to the bay. Tourists and locals flowing through the gardens regularly turned into constant foot traffic. Ruth loved going to the garden with Anne. Today they all enjoyed it together. She remembered a quote by Albert Einstein to look deep into nature to understand everything better. That quote stuck with her because even though she remained an atheist, she would say nature is church. Ruth didn't believe in God anyway, but when her daughter became very ill, she needed someone to vent her anger towards. God, only relevant because something bad happened. That logic did not wash. Dumbfounded by the catastrophe that struck their lives then vanished. Admission to the gardens remained free for members like them. It remained a vibrant place with committees, trustees, and advisors. Mother's Day exhibitions, musical events, galas and collaboration with other countries took place. It maintained the world's biggest collection of orchids. Her favorite place to go, the favorite place for Anne with its tropical plants, waterfall, and ecosystem.

Anne took part in a summer program including a sensory center with activities she did with her mom. Outdoor activities were for developing fine and gross motor skills. Many people just ambled around. The heat of the day became intense and the garden provided a canopy and retreat from the humidity. The bay breezes made their way through the trees and foliage as families participated in activities. The lagoon looked so inviting and some pathways, covered with canopies and flowers in every direction. Her daughter cured, changed her entire perspective on life as if she became a completely different person. The sound of water in the background babbled underneath towering oaks. People stare and get lost in the abundance of nature just in one spot. The epiphytes abound and the Spanish moss hung from the oak trees like drapes. Anne stared at the fish in the Koi pond and nearby chameleons darted in and out of the greenery.

Ruth, a broad mixture of emotions, her anger succumbed to her relief that her daughter got better instantly. She didn't want to get caught up in a dramatic delusion and she was happy and that was unfamiliar. Her husband called it an unfamiliar good. She didn't want to come across overboard, a controlled elation inside. She was guarded about how ecstatic she wanted to be. Ruth didn't want to come off as a fool and her magical thinking, if she became too happy, her daughter's illness would resurface. Having flashbacks and being hypervigilant, now common in her demeanor when she mixed in relief and exhaled.

Ruth now approached life with cautious optimism. They walked through the gazebo and by the banyan trees. Being here became a nature bath for the family. They went to the waterfall every time, the most soothing relaxing place for Ruth and her family. The water continuously flowed and looked majestic. Anne seemed to be the one least affected by leukemia. She brushed it off when healed and had more energy and looked much more animated. Kids gathered at the waterfall. Ann internalized a silent self- consciousness. The hospital provided some services for her to be with other kids, but in a hospital setting. Now healthy, her esteem skyrocketed and joy beamed on her face. Other kids seemed drawn to Anne and this made her happy. Before with Anne, it hurt her that other kids stayed away from her in somewhat of a passive ostracization. They crossed the rope bridge together into an opening in the tree cover to allow the wind from the ocean to travel by them as they walked.

A quiet place for everyone and a person's attention remained on their communication with nature more than with each other. Two kids stood together at the waterfall. People stared at the waterfall that put a person in a trance just by staring at it like it connected to something deep inside each person. Rarely did anyone pass by and not stop. Kids reached over the fence to try and touch the waterfall. A young girl stood around the waterfall with her arm around her little sister. Anne made her way to the waterfall as well. Groups toured the gardens. It being summer, more kids than usual showed up during the day. They liked escaping the intense Florida heat.

Several little kids from those families jetted over to the waterfall. All the parents stayed back just enough to give their children the space for wonderment that nature provided so effortlessly. All of the parents looked at each other and their children lovingly. The children hung out with each other and at the waterfall without an agenda. They wouldn't be worrying about hospital bills, school, about what might happen to them, the future or the past.

Ruth stared at them. In a trance herself. In a new respite from worry, she let herself relax. She used to resist the moments. As a child, she didn't worry about the future. Her mind contemplated moments in her past that flowed by her conscience like museum pieces. So many fretful days passed her by and now she was drying off from the storm of caring for what she thought was her dying daughter. It was like her daughter was new and she was new. She held so much anger towards God, but she didn't believe in him and her logic collapsed. She tried to make her daughter well to no avail. The drama filled her days and was siphoning off her ability to be connected to herself and life. She hadn't known grounded in forever. A torrid of emotions swirled in her like the waves in the dream. Still stunned from the dream that expelled her torment.

All of her decisions surrounded her daughter. Constantly drained, preoccupation with all the stories her mind made up while she was trying to save her daughter took her away from the present moment. It was okay. Paul was understanding and supportive and if anything, he made the ride easier for her because of his steadiness. He was her touchstone. She was never close to her parents like she needed to be when she was a child.

Ruth allowed others to love her with all the bitterness in her. The affirmations and understanding of parents, friends and hospital staff kept her tethered to the ground sometimes when she was not freaking out. She always wanted a child of her own and it seemed like that child was going to be taken away. If she believed in God, she would ask him to take her instead. Then her logic collapsed again. She must believe in God to be mad at him and for God to take her instead. Respite enveloped her like like being in the clouds on a jet. She let go and trusted. A new life emerged and she couldn't stop what happened before, she would not be able to stop the moments ahead.

She understood that other parents went through the same thing and then lost their kids and did not want to tempt life with her anger anymore and joy was breaking through like narrow little sunbeams in an afternoon sky. They seemed barely aware of the time when they weren't in their heads trying to figure out life. You must be like a child to enter the kingdom of heaven came to Ruth. Getting from an adult frame of mind to a child's frame of mind was no easy task. Children seemed to be able to trust their conscience so easily without knowing they too were gifted with a conscience. Adults possessed so much stuff in their heads and simplicity evaded them. Children hovered in their simplicity like skipping rocks on a pond. Adults fell into the water like a heavy stone lost in thought clouds and detached from their hearts.

Kids at the waterfall suddenly shifted their feet simultaneously. A cluster now of children focused on something. As all the parents enjoyed watching their kids play and being together and then something changed. The parents didn't see anything different. They collectively started moving toward their children without panic.

The children stared at something like another world. All of the parents looked at each other dumbfounded. No one sensed any danger. Some of the kids reached out and up extending themselves towards something just above them. What it made it odd to them, that none of them remembered ever being in a situation with other parents and children like this. Their children showed bright expressions on their faces. Only a little border on the walkway separated them from the water. The parents placed their hands on their children to keep them from walking straight into the water. Collectively they looked like they stood in a trance. Their parents halfway in a trance and halfway back, in reality, hanging onto their kids. The kids appeared happy like in a mother's arms at peace and rest. Joy covered their faces as the parents continued to be mesmerized. Suddenly it all stopped and the parents looked relieved and dumbfounded at the same time. "What is it?! What do you see?!"

Ruth said out loud to Anne. Anne looked at her mom and pointed back to the waterfall saying "it was the lady" in her little four-year-old voice. Ruth was about to faint. A burst of unmeasurable love filled the air. She absorbed an intense and enormous amount of love. Tears started rolling down her face before she gave them a thought and the parents did their due diligence and gathered their kids like ducklings wondering what on earth just happened. Her daughter started to wrap her arms around her legs and peace washed over them like a waterfall from above and within their hearts. Parents began to scatter. For hours tears made their way down her cheeks. A joy that permeated everything horizon to horizon.

Chapter Twenty-Three: **All Things New**

A spiritual seismic activity surrounded the epicenter of what happened in the garden. All of the children told their parents with identical descriptions. "Pretty lady", "woman with a smile", "she wore a blue and white dress with a very bright light coming from her heart", "peaceful lady", "her dress made of light" just some of the descriptions the children gave to their parents. The parents contacted Father Francis at the church. Social media buzzed as this gave a somewhat covert way for parents to discuss what their children observed that afternoon. Movies came out some fifty years ago on this topic about kids seeing the Virgin Mary. It seemed so far out then and it held its place of relevance in the world far removed from the mainstream conversation. Now she received messages almost daily about ongoing apparitions. A map on the internet displayed all the locations of reported apparitions in the world. Is she a celestial mother who is looking after her children? The whole thing jumped to that level in days. People had shown up and prayed and the staff in charge of the botanical gardens stewed about how to prevent a public relations nightmare. The parents tried to protect their families so they would not be going public with what their children reported. The parents didn't want to bring attention to their families and they tried to protect their privacy. Some parents talked to Father Francis, shared things on social media, talked about it with their closest friends, which moved it to the next level. The gardens personnel tried to keep things business as usual. People generally respected the sanctity of the gardens. Did Mary appear to children because of their innocence? A rumor surfaced that a young girl suddenly became healed from Leukemia.

Ruth rested back at home. She and Paul stayed up late more often talking about what happened. Those became the deepest and most spiritual conversations in her life. They talked about Anne seeing that lady again and being healed of Leukemia as Ruth fought off her last atheistic beliefs.

She told her husband again and again how she thought she would burst. Her daughter being healed and what took place inside her soul. Gratitude sprouted out of her towards a God she never believed in and cursed. She experienced shame for her beliefs and a benediction at the same time. A storm battered her and her family and then in one day, it disappeared. The aftermath, love, simplicity, and clarity. Like a boat tied to a dock with a rope, she understood the length of her spiritual distance from God. Now she wanted to thank God for what happened. She wanted to go back to the waterfall for herself in secret. Her private investigation began and she went to the spot where Anne witnessed the lady. Anne and Paul went to the grocery store together. Curious onlookers inconspicuously went to the gardens posing as nature lovers.

Ruth wanted to talk up her daughter and the healing that took place. She remembered weeping and weeping. Everything happened like a movie trailer as scenes flashed in her mind and the museum pieces of her conscience came forth in a rush. Ruth found herself back at the gardens the next day. It did not become an atmosphere of chaos, but of serene calmness. Something changed about the location. An attraction for obvious reasons, but now a larger than normal crowd gathered. Calm came on her like it did the other day. She must go by herself. She needed to have her one on one with God or whoever showed up in front of her daughter and now the other kids. It did not getting out of hand turning in part from a garden to a grotto.

A sense of peace began to wash over her like a rain shower that was turning into a downpour. No one seemed to notice and she didn't care if anyone was watching her. To everyone else, she thought she looked like a woman having a solitary moment. Paul and Anne showed up after all to surprise mommy. They didn't see her yet. The tears began to run down her face and immense love filled every fiber of her being. The giant finger of God was touching her soul. She fell into a trance just like her daughter did two times before. A very bright light appeared and out of that light a lady approached. Miraculously, she did not have to shield her eyes. A most beautiful lady appeared to her as Ruth's soul was now rapturous. Ruth venerated the holy being in front of her, her soul was being cleansed. The lady kept her gaze down and her hands stretched out as if to allow light to flow through her. Her gown was blue and white. Now appeared flickers of gold all around her like flames of the brightest possibility. She folded her arms over her chest and maintained the most beautiful continence. Below the lady appeared a host of angels who slowly opened their wings from what they covered and revealed, a very vivid image of Jesus on the cross lashed and tortured beyond description. His entire body wounded. The blood covered his entire body and the skin over his knees was raw as if dragged endlessly. He appeared striped with wounds as the angels closed their wings to cover Jesus up. They disappeared and Mary now looked up at Ruth with the gentlest look imaginable. A gaze of unparalleled peace and serenity. She suddenly receded into heaven and everything in the garden came back into her concentration. Paul and Anne stood next to her and people looked at her not knowing what to think. Her conversion was complete. She was the most unique and noble person that Ruth ever encountered. Grief left her soul as if siphoned out of her. The tears helped rinse off the collage of sadness built into her by her suffering and the omnipotence of God casted aside any doubt. A gem of holiness appeared before Ruth's eyes. Mary was nothing for the sake of herself. Ruth was consoled and experienced the superabundant goodness of God. She understood that Mary was Jesus' mother and her very own. A scripture lanced her consciousness when Jesus told John to behold his mother. At home, she noticed the magazine that her daughter pointed to in the grocery store.

Chapter Twenty Four: **The Litany**

K iana looked at Catholic Television that aired a story about the alleged sightings from children in South Florida. Total dedication and solemnity, her brands of being in the world. Her faith and inner world sustained her. Kiana built her foundation on God and the storm did come. Like the stabilized flag pole in the image of Iwo Jima, she stood upright amidst personal devastation. She experienced her conversion as a child being brought into the Catholic faith by her parents. Her father died twenty years ago and succumbed to cancer while her mother outlived him and died only five years ago of old age. Jesus remained her mom's best friend. This became a signature moment in her life because even though she believed in God her whole life and spent her life going to mass, Kiana realized at that moment that much of her life more of an identification with the Catholic faith than a relationship with any one person. The idea of a holy family consoled her.

Kiana said her prayers in earnest and said them diligently. She consistently said prayers all the time with their whole heart in it. Her faith waxed and waned just like anyone else. A great friend who lost her husband before Kiana lost hers told her she lived in so much grief that she couldn't pray. She maintained a group of friends whom she met with once a week who would share what they read. It became a book club without everyone reading the same book, but instead, her friends shared ideas about their book selections. It stood as an enriching wellspring of bonding with her sisters as she liked to call them. They shared losses in their circle. Husbands, children, and friends passed away and so they all shared many things in common. They talked about their marriages, their children and their friendships continued as a source of strength and sustenance. When Kiana lost her husband, she fell into a well of despair and even deeper recently when Tracy died in a car crash suddenly. These losses moved her relationship with a God from a place of worship of someone who lived far away in heaven to one in her very heart. The tabernacle of her heart became occupied by God.

Being a devout Catholic made her familiar with the rosary that she prayed every day. She started each morning with that prayer with all her intentions. She tried to meditate on all the mysteries of the day. Somedays the words barely made their way out of her mouth and other days she prayed with strength. She realized her frailty as a human.

She followed the Medjugorje apparitions. She didn't birddog news stories from the site, she just checked in from time to time. The Immaculate Concepcion, something about that title that esteemed and venerated the mother of Jesus like no other. Her life became a walk with Mary who always talked up her son. That phrase stuck out to her. Many of the books that she read covered Jewish and Christian mysticism. Even though she remained Catholic, she developed curiosity about other people and what they believed. Buddhism interested her as a let go and move on approach to life. It seemed to be an everything in moderation mantra as she read in the bible. She and Trevor shared the same level of curiosity. The main differences, that he didn't want to be religious and she loved being unabashedly religious. Both equally curious yet ages apart. Kindred as a mother and son. Now Tracy's best friend became a solace and a son for her. Kiana did become like a mentor for him as he searched for something spiritual that would be an anchor in his life without formal membership. Kiana thought of it all as one big family.

Everything would come out in the wash. Right now, God put her on tumble. She remembered a pope saying that "Jesus didn't come down off of his cross and I'm not coming down off of mine." Kiana waited for a smaller cross. To her, the Marian apparitions appeared as a common occurrence and she read about them for years now. She knew people with extreme fanatical beliefs and she stayed away from that energy. To her modesty, remained a key ingredient. Her life stood as a litany to God. She devoted and consecrated herself to Jesus and Mary as her mother once told her, "you know, if Jesus and Mary are on your side, you can't lose." The church didn't yet approve of these sightings as it normally took a hundred years for an apparition site to be approved. One thing that stood out to her, the sheer number of times Mary has been appearing as of now, 30 million people visited the site over the course of 20 years. "Live my Son" and "conversion to God is for every day" she read. A personal encounter is something she longed for in her life. Through the internet, knowledge increased exponentially throughout the world daily because of technology. Distractions from keeping the eye on the prize, the kingdom of God within her.

She didn't need the church's blessing and she thought it would only be a matter of time. The place became an international reference point for conversions. People claimed to sense the presence of Mary. She believed God reached out to people through the Virgin. Despite all the criticism, a million people a year visited the site in Eastern Europe. Doubts and thoughts of delusion made their way into people's minds as well. Orphans, women in crisis, the disabled, drug addicts and all those in need showed up. Kiana believed that the mother of God to be present at the center of it all.

Trevor came by to check on her as Kiana came to be a mother to him and she always cooked good food to eat. She let Trevor take any of Tracy's items that he wanted. As she looked to the holy family, Trevor looked at Kiana's family as a model and ideal of a family. He told her it is the best chicken he ever ate. She got the recipe from some farm girl in Iowa off the internet. He casually mentioned to her, "you know the rumors continue of the story around a botanical garden Florida" Kiana looked up at him in surprise as she enjoyed the birds in the bird feeder on her back porch. A hummingbird flew right past Trevor's face as he leaned back. "So, you say" Kiana replied. "What do you think? Think it might be true", Trevor asked? "Maybe," said Kiana. "Get this. A woman who being reportedly an atheist witnessed an apparition of Mary. Here is the kicker. A little girl who suffered from leukemia miraculously became healed and that girl is the woman's daughter. What do you think? Would you go ? " Trevor postulated. Kiana searched her intuition elated by the question.

Chapter Twenty Five: **In the News Today**

R on lived as a closet Catholic, intrigued by the mass, stories about saints, The Blessed Mother's role in God's plan and history in the bible. A quick short report came on the television as he lay half passed out on the couch after finishing off a bowl of butter popcorn. People talked about a woman, who would not come forward about experiences at a garden not far from his doorstep. Many people talked about her daughter experiencing miraculous healing in the garden and the mother later reported a trance-like experience. The only consistent piece of news being that her daughter reported a pretty lady whom the child identified when seeing a magazine about Mary in a local grocery store. Ron also bought the same magazine. He read where a saint said that Mary shows people to heaven like a sailor using a star and that St. Paul started the first Marianist church. Approximately a dozen apparitions have been approved by the church. He vetted the whole apparition thing. Going to that place so close by now sewed into his intuition. An ever-present place on the map of his consciousness.

A crowd of believers started to gather. Several children at the site at the same time observed a beautiful lady in a blue mist right in front of a waterfall. The sense of serenity and sacredness drew him in. Somehow that spirit deep within him could see that. His devotional told him that Jesus lived at his center amidst the doubts, distractions, and rapidity of everyday life. The story surfaced outside the mainstream. As all of the information news-wise on his phone reported about incidental things that happen locally, nationally and around the world. As a kid he remembered that the news came on at 6:30p every night for a half hour. The Apparitions he heard about were from parishioners on the occasions when his foster parents would take him to church. The world, on the whole, found people busy with their lives so much so that even now a very small portion of people of the earth attended them. That being said, Medjugorje experienced 30 million visitors in 20 years. Ron thought that it could just be a placebo. This being the skeptic in him.

Ron understood Mary didn't want to be worshiped but venerated. Since the botanical gardens were so close he could drive in ninety minutes by car. Ron's emotional need for a celestial mother he found in Mary. For him, she puts a feminine face on God. To him, she would be the bridge between religions. He talked to many people about God, so many religions and denominations and remembered the time Quinn told him "don't go Catholic on me." The gardens remained beautiful and he enjoyed the best scallops near at a local restaurant.

Ron experienced an anonymous upbringing. He wondered if other kids went through the same things as him. His parents didn't notice him and he didn't want their attention because they became so unavailable in their addiction. He always tried to be dutiful. Since he is older than his brother, he took on the hero role in the family. Quinn played the role of mascot and always cut up and got into trouble.

Ron remained an orphan long after birth and now encouraged that a pope said that "a Christian without the Madonna is an orphan." He always put so much pressure on himself to do things right. He tried to be the hero and now divorced with a broken family. Ron was lost and he experienced the most difficult time moving forward because he faced such a hard time connecting to people. Ron tried to find himself in between his parents, but when they drank, a storm of all their wounds gushed like Lava. Quinn never idealized a father. He bounced around so much like a sports team he used to joke about it going from one foster home to the next and became used to being on the road so to speak. Nurturing didn't occur much at home. He used to go to the local YMCA. Not one to ask for help when stressed out, he started jogging in high school and then gave it up for a long time. Then one day he started with two miles, then four, up to ten, twelve and he got to the point where twenty became doable. It turned into his drug. He purged the anxiety in him like opening a drain and did this regularly in nature as he hated treadmills because they were boring. Body, mind, and spirit came together for him when he went out in nature. He processed so much of his childhood and life and it became his free therapy. After a while, his body started sending him tabs as his heel gave him problems as well as his knee. He loved running in the rain.

Somehow, he knew God worked on that with him. He was lonely with no one to share his feelings with except his friend at the sports bar. He judged himself a failure with the end of his marriage. The thing that scared him to death though, his parents exploding and drinking. It drove him crazy. He always tried to make the best decisions because he wanted their approval so bad. The lens of his heart began to open. Ron allowed God to occupy his heart more and more. Surrendering took the pressure off.

Ron tried to find a way to speak his truth more often and say what he meant. It remained one of his many challenges with his faith. His heart said what his words couldn't. Part of him concluded going to the garden would be crazy. This stayed on his heart and his intuition. His conscience and inner wisdom were telling him to go. He opened his magazine that he got at the grocery store to the page inside that contained a picture of Fatima at night on May 13. The countless number of people with their glowing lights could be seen. That energy drew him in like a vacuum, the excitement like a storm chaser as he reached for his suitcase again. He went crazy the time his brother faded away and this time he would go to where all of his doubts would fade away quickly.

Chapter Twenty Six: **New World**

Ruth's world blown to smithereens. In the former life when Anne became very ill she tried so very hard as she wrestled to believe in God. She switched allegiance from one team to another. A message for her as she threw all her punches at God without even connecting one of them. They all came back to her exasperated spirit and with each blow, she became wearier while trying to be a statue of serenity for her daughter. Her husband stood by her while the boat rocked back and forth like the dream. She experienced the epiphany that the dream became the spiritual parallel to what she went through. All made sense to her now and the gravity with which she understood God stunned her. The burning question, not why all this happened, but rather instead what she learned from God. The curtain between her and God now truly torn. The mysteries of God remained too many and an unsolvable riddle.

Here is her life however like a mast being the only thing standing after a typhoon of adversity. Anne remained the strongest one of all with her heart always as light as a feather. Her daughter no longer trapped in the world of duality and not accumulating all the judgments and knowledge that a parent deals with on their own. Her daughter became closer to God by not thinking about God because she always went about her way without calculating right and wrong. Since Ruth being the opposite, everything calculated and of course, she thought God punished her and abandoned her at the same. Even that to her became a logic that left the reality of the present moment skewed.

The psychic tension that she wore her whole life seemed to be a heavy jacket one size too small. They all laid and lounged in their living room watching a kids' movie as Ruth looked at Anne and Paul with gratitude. Happiness found her like a child wrapped in a mother's arms. Little did she understand that she and Anne shared the same feeling. Paul would not to waiver in the storm and he remained the steadiness of Ruth's journey. Paul saw Ruth contrived to find ways to make her relationship with God a boxing match. Each punch she threw only served to wear her out even more and with each one, she fought her way to her surrender. Insecurity provoked her to find answers and to hate the heavy lifting in her spirit. The Holy Spirit told her to rest and the beauty of her spirit blossomed like the solstice of spring. The might of God like a parent telling a child to settle down and be quiet. How the apparition affected her, like a parent snatching a child running across a busy street. The words in her soul that day, spoken in silence as to "stay close to me." The strikingly beautiful and serene Madonna visited her.

Ruth won a spiritual lottery, but the money was God's and she waited to see what she would be told what to do. From heaven, she would make her next withdrawal. She went back to the garden. Mary said yes to God. Ruth said no to God her whole life. Her life as she knew ended and her real-life began. Contemplation became her new course. Her life would be public, but her peace, family and sanity would be protected in seclusion under the mantle of Mary.

The passive resistance approach worked for the public relations people at the gardens. They walked on rice paper to keep the integrity and function of the gardens intact. Little did Ruth understand the science behind nature sounds. In the tumult of the last year. The gardens didn't want a bunch of religious freaks or zealots showing up and turning their kingdom upside down. Something to do with the level of attachment the person held to that belief system. Ruth kidded with herself before about being religiously atheistic in her life. The whole time she would rise in the morning and take care of her daughter. When she wanted to walk she went to the beach or the gardens to walk. When she wanted to sit, she would go to the beach or the gardens to sit.

Ruth went out to nature to refuel so to speak. The gardens remained her church. A pure relaxation took over her as she listened to the sounds. She liked the trees with those big leaves rustling in the wind and went to Maine once and heard the leaves in the bitter cold wind. She loved the waterfall in the children's rainforest. Science remained her religion. Her body and mind restored every time. So many times, she wanted to give up. The synapses started being changed in her brain when she looked at the foliage. Neuron connections optimized while the cortisol decreased in her fight or flight instinct that stayed on overdrive for so long.

The running water and the birds in the trees provided the nature sounds that helped her become peaceful and content. She loved wherein she read about research that measured brain waves and heart rate of those exposed to nature sounds. Ruth just needed space to enjoy these sounds and her brain enjoyed the relaxation that nature brought to her. Every time she went to the gardens her heart rate shifted along with her entire nervous system. Acute stress embedded in her from all the worry. The sympathetic responses of her body declined when she went to nature and her adrenal glands became less reactive. The catecholamines contained adrenaline and non adrenaline. When stressed, she took shorter breaths and this became the way she lived her life. She dove to the bottom of the ocean of despair. Her blood vessels constricted.

The homeostasis of her body, out of control as she didn't rest and digesting her food became challenging. Her daughter had been sick and her parasympathetic nervous system went haywire. The fight and flight of her sympathetic nervous system left her fight or flight in disarray. Ruth, dismantled from the inside out. Ruth's unconscious acts of breathing, digesting and the ability to prepare for a nap became compromised. She lived in the hospital all the time with her daughter and central nervous system would not relax and allow her to get connected to her inner peace. When they came to the gardens, it cleaned the temple of the body. Disconnecting from all that stress became paramount to her survival. Doctor visits and medical treatments for her daughter kept her engaged at a rapid energetic pace. Hypervigilance wore her out.

Ruth wasn't productive at all with being a stay at home mom with a very ill daughter. She was in react mode almost all the time and she was alone even with her husband present. Without him, she would fall apart. He was helping keep the family together by being steady. He had been agnostic his whole life so by not attaching himself to any specific belief system he was able to keep his emotions in check. Paul did, however, believe in a divine intelligence in nature with all the sophisticated order and patterns that underlined everything in nature. Common ground he had with Ruth and something that they both believed in. Much of their recreational time was spent outside when possible. He wasn't strong enough to cure Anne's leukemia and so together they longed for something more powerful.

Being exposed to nature sounds with all of her high-stress levels enabled her to have somewhat of a positive attitude when being confronted with the difficulties of her daughter's illness. She came to the gardens with

Paul and Anne and sometimes with just Anne and experienced a significant drop in tension and Paul noticed that she was much less irascible when they came home from the gardens. A rupture had taken place in their family because of leukemia. They bonded together to support each other even though the stress on the parents was monumental. Anne somehow was the one who was the real trooper throughout the whole ordeal.

A rupture was taking place in America on the whole. People used their devices in nature to see how far they walked or to measure their current heart rate. Technology and nature may be used together. Technology can help us understand nature with all its accessible information at the touch of a finger. To the same degree, Ruth realized that they were not the same.

Ruth was aware that human beings and nature were real energy while technology was artificial energy. She often talked about the disruption of natural energy between humans by artificial energy or even artificial intelligence. This created challenges for humans to connect to nature because their receptivity of vibrations in the universe was now interrupted by artificial energy.

People end up choosing one or the other. Technology helped her to understand her daughter's illness at an advanced level of knowledge. Spending time in the woods or in nature was important and way more interesting. She loved the sign that said Nature: No Wi-Fi, but we guarantee a better connection. Technology didn't connect, but disconnected. There existed harmony in nature for her. Technology did help to make life safer in ways as a preventative factor to improve the health of people around the world. Her instinct to return to nature and get rid of technology would not go away. She concluded that we need nature to function.

She was able to focus with the symphony of nature. Nature was just in our DNA and no matter how much we became technologically advanced, she needed that close connection with nature, which is the very source of energy that powers the planet. She passed by Eli once on her way out of the garden. "This is how God is taking care of you," he said. The words hit her today like a giant epiphany of wisdom that had been bubbling in her spirit. She realized that she had been staring at God the whole time.

Chapter Twenty Seven: **A Large Crowd**

The children who went to the garden reported having smelled roses during the apparition. People began to gather at the gardens after the parents gathered their children. One child reportedly said to her parents that the lady promised to send the Holy Spirit. Children murmured to their parents in wonderment after their parents snatched them away from the location. The children clustered together when they witnessed the apparition. Parents looked up apparitions on the internet while the kids shared things on their minds. The parents, described as a controlled panic. Occurring was the introduction of something holy. Their environment, altered spiritually and physically. A physiological reaction began in the parents as their egos resisted what their children shared. The first word out of every parents' mouth, "what"?! The better the quality of the relationship between parent and child, the more the child would tell them. Each parent thought their kid became certifiably crazy and didn't want to risk anyone thinking that they maybe lost it themselves. The interrogations began and lasted throughout the rest of the day. The expressions on all the kids' faces remained the same. An expression of intense joy remained an understatement. Parents couldn't help themselves with too much to contain and they began peeping it out to family members and friends. The ivy grew faster. Some people in leadership positions expressed fury about these events taking place in their gardens. God seeks no one's permission for anything. Most people tried to fit it all into their very own scheme of things. Some people showed up to pray and this appeared off-putting to some who looked at flowers and enjoy the scenery. People prayed the rosary openly without trying to disturb anyone else. The uninvited events, God's version of crashing the party. What the perfect spot in the gardens next to the ocean. Mother nature and divine energy at the best location. People with no spiritual attachments found it all odd and eccentric. The gardens tried to stay relevant as a botanical magnet for those who wanted to learn more about nature. Those onlookers of the Catholic flock and their close relatives watched very intently. People by the scores now were on the precipice like they leaned on the glass at the zoo to get a closer look without participating. No one wanted to be that person who appeared a fool and make the mistake of falling for something false.

The challenge for everyone would be like a teenager who grew up in one place though emotionally they pined for the old neighborhood. Accepting the suchness of the present moment challenged every human being. A person always seems to be held by the past or future. When every single person expressed a concern about what stirred, they worried about the future or keeping the past as the past. The subtle shock of it all, that somehow everyone cohabitated together. No riots and neither a sign held high took place. It became a vigil, a memorial, and a sacred location. Like someone who moved a few rocks in a brook, the water flowed around the immovable object. The parking lot remained full. People of course still paid admission regardless of why they came, but that, however, didn't become the surmounting issue. The children's waterfall appeared as ground zero and this many people never appeared in the garden before. The crowd remained quiet and manageable. They assembled peacefully to almost everyone's surprise. The operations team of the garden still thought plenty of people came to the garden specifically for what it provided, a place to be with and learn about nature. Maybe that remained part of the whole point of it all. People began to make assumptions and connections that somehow if something holy occurred, it would be about God and nature or the same. The natural sounds among the water, trees, birds and anything else that made noise affected the bodily systems that control the flight or flight response, the rest-digest autonomic nervous system and the overall resting activity of the brain. The sounds and sights of the garden promoted relaxation and well-being.

The purpose, to recall that Jesus is alive, loved everyone and to emphasize that without God, mankind is lost. Some people would put it as insane. The miracles drew attention to that message. People listened to sounds from the natural environment and their autonomic nervous system and heart rates changed when they visited the garden. The natural sounds in the garden itself kept everyone from focusing on themselves. Their brains connecting with natural sights and sounds reflected outward-focused attention. Somehow artificial sounds and noise and their brain activity reflected an inward focus of attention. This contributed to people becoming anxious, depressed and even traumatized. The self is the biggest problem that people face. People focused like addicts to their devices. The more attention they paid to nature, the calmer they became and the better they paid attention.

Interest in the overall effects of environmental exposure among physical and mental health settings grew. The environment and natural world made its way into issues of public health and town planning. Somehow nature made its way into behavioral, physiological and brain exploration. So far people religious, spiritual or not classified the apparitions as "not worthy of belief", "not contrary to faith" or "worthy of belief." It took all kinds of people to make up the place. Everyone possessed a mind that wondered and being in the garden allowed people to be task free. It seemed like they appeared to be in default wakefulness. Some couldn't help to be on their phones still checked out and make themselves less available to mother nature. It seemed that on the whole and because of technology, people held an inward focus that included worrying, ruminating about themselves and linking themselves to psychological stress. People quickly responded to nature more than the artificial sounds involving technology.

All the numbers of people increased and without a second thought, immersed themselves in nature. Most people didn't understand that being in nature reduced anger as well as fears and stress. It didn't have all the intensity of a theme park with its crowds and stress mixed with fun and exhilaration. When people came to the gardens, it stood as a medicine for all peoples by improving physical well-being, reducing blood pressure, heart rate, muscle tension and the production of stress hormones. Some people believed that it reduced mortality. Even in hospitals, schools, and offices, a single plant can reduce anxiety. No wonder Ruth kept coming back to the gardens. She came here as much for herself as she did for Anne. Not only Ruth but people, in general, experienced decreased heart rates and shifting in their body's autonomic nervous system response. Even the nature sounds decreased the fight or flight feelings. The parasympathetic nervous systems of people became affected too as the natural surroundings of the garden helped relax the rest-digest responses in the body. The more stressed people became, the more the effect. Artificial sounds didn't have the same effect on the body.

The gardens helped Anne deal with the discomfort and pain from the leukemia treatment. She and her mother gravitated genetically to find trees, plants, water and were engrossed in the natural elements. The gardens absorbed them and distracted them from their pain and discomfort. Ruth loved to learn about nature and the science of it, her religion. So here is how she had a buy-in. She read where people who viewed trees from their hospital rooms tolerated pain better and spent less time in the hospital. By coming to the garden so often she tried to find a way to heal her daughter beyond medicine. She tried to be hopeful while bringing Anne here. What she learned and what people didn't understand is that the more people are around green spaces the stronger feelings of unity with others, and had strong feelings of belonging. The now spiritual underpinnings at the garden became a greater sense of community. The community and divine point to be made became bigger than this. In turn, this reduced the risk of street crime, reducing violence and aggression and increased the capacity to cope with poverty and life's demands. Even though their daughter had insurance, they still faced costs associated with the leukemia treatment that put a serious lien on their finances.

When people came to the garden out of curiosity about the reports they heard, they became surprised at how beautiful it appeared. The part of their brains associated with the empathy and love lit up. Somehow their fears and anxiety became reduced at the same time. People connected with their environment while they investigated the supernatural.

What they didn't understand as well, it is deadly to have too much time in front of screens. The technology did more than ever and increased in fascination. Depression made its way into their lives decreasing their ability to have empathy and help others. People became more isolated and indifferent. They deprived themselves of time in the natural world. This became associated with a higher risk of death. Nature remained Ruth's haven. The gardens stood as the nature bath that optimized nervous system functions, balanced heart conditions and reduced digestive disorders. Ruth was content that she found respite in nature that helped people with their eyesight and she read where kids who play outside have better eyesight than kids who don't.

The whole place had become an enigma. Everyone went to the gardens as a family or by themselves and they left healthier for it. BMI reduced in people who did their exercising outdoors, they are less fatigued and suffer less from obesity and related conditions. What got Ruth's attention, when she learned that being in nature stimulated the production of anti-cancer proteins. Walking in nature improved a lot of aging people's attention because they reported that they had better memories than people in urban environments. Ruth wanted to have a job at the gardens she loved it so much. It became helpful to people's moods when they suffered from depression.

The cortisol in her body went to an all-time high at various times in Anne's treatment and mother nature helped to lower her blood pressure. Those who ran the gardens knew nature improved creative abilities heightened while being in nature more than being on electronic devices. She applied that to nature even though she wasn't old at all. People look at animals or nature she thought because they are uncomplicated. Medicines and treatments complicated her life. It slowed her mind down as it did everyone who came to the gardens. Nature had a way of doing that as well as lifting her mood out of depression and gave her more energy.

For some reason, nature helped people pay attention longer and perform better on tasks. People became better problem solvers and became more creative. Her senses came alive when she went outside. She couldn't help, but be filled with gratitude. Being cranky had become a way of life for her since her daughter had become ill. The judge in her head told her she shouldn't be happy if her daughter is ill. It would look bad. She read in a study that mood disorders are on the increase and this correlates with people living more in urban centers. This affected urban planning.

She told her husband about her dream and about the apparition at the gardens. He believed every word she said without question. She now realized the whole time that God had been helping her by bringing her here while she carried her cross. The crowds became much bigger now at the gardens. The upside for those running the place is that they had a huge boost in revenue and interest. They held their breath. People assembled peacefully.

People adapted to things better in the natural environment compared to human-made habitats. Somehow the natural light had positive effects on their stress, blood pressure, and immune systems. People being in the space of nature made them much more aware of their environment. This would forever be a sacred space for her. One older lady approached her and told her that she had a beautiful light around her. This, one of the nicest things anyone has ever said to her. Ruth understood that somehow people connected to their identity with nature. The large numbers of people coming to the gardens became generalizable to the whole population as people became less egocentric in nature and their language changed as well. The global uptake in technological advancement did make people's lives easier in a countless number of ways.

Ruth wanted to apply for a job at the gardens because she could spend her entire day there. She agreed with the research that pointed to lower stress levels, lower heartbeats, and pulse rates. Overall general stress declined for people in nature. She felt blessed to be able to be so close to the beach as well. Even staring at the clouds made her happy like a little kid. All the negative emotions from her daughter's leukemia had nearly taken every bit of energy from her. She had been seeing articles about how nature added to one's sense of self, others and toward Mother Nature. Her marriage got a much-needed breath of fresh air. Ruth bought a devotional and read today the part about you do not have because you do not ask.

The Holy Spirit told her that mankind suffers from unhappiness because we have disconnected from nature and if we just look around we would see evidence of God everywhere. The breach between man and nature or God and mankind is leading to a spiritual crisis globally. The truth of who we are is hidden in nature and our material gains have blinded us and broke us. Lonely and unhappy people turned more and more to technology and the consequence became gloom.

It became a major blow to her ego to see that God had been with her all along and that all this goodness and the sanctity of a person. Before Anne got sick they used to go on walks together as a family and she tried her luck at gardening. She grew up near farmland as a child. Ruth wondered how old people looked so peaceful especially the groundskeeper she kept seeing every time she came to the gardens. He looked old and young to her at the same time. She had never seen anything like it and noticed that people seemed to be more relaxed here and they spoke to each other more.

She loved how the sunshine made silhouettes with the leaves against the sky. The sun always made her healthier. The vitamin D prevented osteoporosis, cancer, diabetes, and cancer in people all around her. She read that technology kept us indoors and we tried to supplement our health with pills. Sunshine, however, the most powerful offense against that deficit. Staring at computer screens all day presented a dilemma for people who would later develop myopia and chronic headaches. Greeneries like the garden remained the natural best solution and she loved how the kids enjoyed being outside. She always remembered their laughter.

She realized that God used the environment to help purify her body of toxins. He straight cured her daughter of leukemia she thought. Ruth wondered what the whole experience might be leading to. She became an expert in nature and realized that spending more time indoors put our respiratory systems at significant risk. Bronchitis and asthma became more common in those who stayed indoors. Nature built a fat burner in people's bodies and helped with their metabolism. This related to longer life spans and fewer health problems.

Nature had been the best healer for her as she found herself clear and awakened outside. she read that people who had connections to landscapes are happier on the inside. For her, people who were happier on the inside were closer to God. Her therapist once told her that the people he had seen who put their spiritual life first became those he had seen do the best in coping with life. They just seemed more balanced, focused and more resilient. Nature, the best medicine. It remained divine energy the whole time.

Chapter Twenty Eight: **We Need To Go**

K iana needed a win spiritually. They shared a long quality marriage that remained a mainstay in her life. She spent time with friends by going to church, having girls' night out. Trevor talked her into flying to where the apparition occurred. Her husband left her well off with his military retirement and life insurance. The fact that she sat on a plane, a huge curveball in her life that she threw herself. She held many darts to throw in her life and this would be one of the last.

Kiana told her friends they loved her so much they were unsurprisingly supportive. Everyone minded their own spiritual business in the sister group. She flew on the plane with Trevor and didn't understand if what he read by mystics to be the actual truth. He appeared spiritual in his nature and that stood as the thing that stood out most to him. She thought about the man in the hospital room when she went. For some reason, he kept popping up in her conscience. This might be a wild goose chase for sure in her mind. She thought that even if nothing appeared, they would at least be able to go to the gardens. "We need to go" Trevor told her as he followed the online story closely and he looked up the social media posts that lit up like crazy. Lots of talk about miracles and children being healed after seeing a beautiful lady.

Skepticism became the first reaction common among humans because why would someone from heaven visit here in the first place? And no one wanted to be a fool for believing in the second place. The more someone believed something like this happened made them subjected to being labeled fanatical, Pentecostal or Catholic weirdo. People became indifferent in this day and age and the internet allowed everyone to dismiss apparitions like artifacts on a glass shelf. Twenty years of apparitions in one place would not be enough to convince the general public. Apparitions have a dramatic effect on people when they went.

Kiana couldn't care less though. Losing her young son, she wanted to die herself. Trevor did his best to keep her from falling. He didn't worry that Kiana would do something drastic, he just didn't want her to fall back any farther. Trevor would check on her regularly and didn't want to play his music as much though at the same time music kept him connected to himself. He kept repeating and repeating what he imagined the whole crash to be and how Kiana had been turned into a zombie with no life in her eyes.

When he played the drums and let himself go, he naturally created patterns powerfully and with finesse. He liked just beating and pounding the drums. Sometimes he would play along to music, practice rudiments and lastly learn about reading music. He liked watching other drummer's styles. After Tracy died, he had to find interest again and so because of his grief his approach to playing became more therapeutic than anything else. The drums became a Zen space for him. His playing also fueled by the fact that his parents divorced due to their fighting, his mom's alcoholism, anorexia, and his dad's explosiveness. He played the role of the peacemaker.

Trevor had his hypersensitivity to not being heard. His parents carried poison around in their minds. His interest in God became a search purely for a benevolent guide. To belong to religion had its benefits. Kiana sat next to him on the flight. He looked out of the window seat into the universe and contemplated all the museum pieces in his mind from his past. He was afraid to lose his parents growing up believing they would abandon him and always afraid of being abused. They didn't hit him, but the screaming a silent torture for an innocent heart. His dad tried to control his mom and his mom clung to him out of her fear. Trevor did his best to hold back all that negativity. No wonder he became easy friends with Tracy and his family. They became the gel he had always been looking for. She was strong, warm, graceful and peaceful. Music and searching for God remained his passions. Religion sought to enclose him from his vantage point. To him, spirituality gave him a very deep pool with no bottom and lots of water. To say he is this or that was to identify with one particular religion and exclude the rest. He didn't have an issue with religion. Trevor remained independent so he would experience greater freedom in his spirituality. The age-old paradigm of it is God and us still held its solid ground. He thought that the impact of religion would dissolve over time and that spirituality would take the most prominent place in the world of beliefs. Growing up centered around no safe place, fear, anger and feeling powerless.

The child in him wanted revenge and when he became friends with Tracy, Kiana loved him like a mom from the start. Being part of Kiana's family gave him a sense of family, but even he realized that this couldn't keep him from grief and loss. Deep down he wanted to be cleansed and healed. This became the root that drove him to purge the poison that had been sent into his mind from his parent's minds. He believed that the apparitions would wash away the effects on him of growing up in the family he did. Remembering his family and mourning how he wished it had gone had been part of his path. Spiritually, he shopped. A window shopper at best. Trevor tried to evolve into a more realistic solution. He will always have to deal with his parents and he wants them to not forget.

At an essential level, he tried to integrate everything he had been through while accepting and healing. Music remained the only thing he bought into because there is no right and wrong in it. It just was. Trevor could always reconnect with himself through the music. His mind processed at a different place like a long-distance runner. Kiana in the seat next to him was a long-distance runner too. Losing her husband and son became races she was still running. In her heart, she collapsed into the arms of her Mother. She kept a mental note that was fascinating to her. She thought isn't it interesting that Jesus was willing to share his mother with us. She bore her pain watching him die on the cross and it appeared nonetheless that when Jesus told John to behold his Mother, Jesus shared his Mother with the entire human race. A celestial ever-present mother. If she had a dollar for every time someone told her that Mary had no power at all and that she was just an ordinary woman. The first time she ever viewed the image of Our Lady of Sorrows, she knew that Mary was very powerful. Later she came to learn that she never could be comfortable or easy if Mary was not nearby. They flew at cruising altitude now. It was like they shared a mission together and for different reasons. A most unlikely pair of people on their way to the place where people said something out of this world had entered.

Kiana's friends gave her mixed reviews. Some remained skeptical and others supportive. She figured that if she was betting that this would be the collection of responses she would receive. She had to fight to not want to die herself. Some things happened to everyone. Jesus, tortured and crucified. What an odd combination she thought to herself for going on this trip with Trevor. This was not any young man. He was her son by proxy as he was as close to Tracy as she could get. The good feelings she had from being around

Trevor counteracted the horror of losing her son. They would go to the gardens the next day and it all appeared like a dream to her.

Every time she read a report she was able to catch a glimmer of hope. Trevor was good at keeping track of things. He was always perusing the internet for interesting things to read. To him, Jesus and The Tao seemed like the same things. Jesus said he was the way and the truth and the life. The Tao, referred to as life. If you strive to connect to it then you lose touch with it. If you try to accord with it, your efforts will be futile. Creation is Jesus smiling. That was his favorite, but the world didn't talk about things in this way. Religions appeared as shoeboxes to him. Different box different shoes. He would be the one to go barefoot and not wear any of the shoes. Being in his bare feet was most comfortable to him. He had the utmost respect for Kiana and that her lifelong faith to be a monument.

Trevor had shared so much about what he had seen story-wise about what was happening at the gardens. He did not want her to be disappointed as she was a glass full of grief. The stories however that he had seen, remarkable, to say the least. A lady converted from atheism after she reported to a confidant that she had seen The Mother of Jesus. Not only that, her daughter was instantly cured of leukemia after being treated for a year and not getting better. Little children had been telling their parents of a lady dressed in blue that smiled at them. Parents were astonished that their kids told them such things with amazing consistency. Kiana imagined what Mary must have gone through, pregnant and couldn't tell anyone. This lady at the gardens who said she did see Mary said something to somebody about what happened. The news spread like wildfire. The press wanted to talk to her and she refused to add doubt and controversy to her story.

Kiana thought children do not lie to get into trouble. He thought her willingness to do a sudden pilgrimage to south Florida testified to something great. The Catholic church did not approve of what had happened because they never made a statement. Father Tony from the local parish was very guarded on the subject because he didn't want to fuel anything among the flock. He was ready to retire and if God wanted to send his Mother somewhere that was up to him. Father Tony was aware that God operated outside the physical laws of science and didn't need men's approval for anything.

They made plans to stay at a local hotel. Kiana trusted Trevor to make all the plans for flying, the hotels, and the rental car. "What are you going to do if we watch an apparition?" said Trevor. "Well," Kiana said, "I put my complete trust in God even when I find that is the hardest thing to do. Everything around us is changing all the time even as we speak, we are aging and getting older. I am willing and just want to be where other people say they have seen Our Lady. Someone could say we are caught up in religion and why are we focusing on Mary? I believe she is a messenger of God like a mom trying to warn her children. Something dire may be close to the human race. Many times, God sent messengers so I am not surprised about that. I think what surprises me is that it is so close here in America. I could use some light in my life because everything hurts so much. If we don't then we will go home and my faith will be the same. I don' t need this to believe. A wicked generation wants a sign. Who are we to think that we will not suffer? Jesus suffered. Mary suffered. We suffer. Each of us carries a cross. Some much bigger than others. It is pure curiosity on my part and hope. I have to admit that it is something. I'm glad we're going. Something will come out of this. I don't think we are going for absolutely nothing. That's what I think."

"I think this is phenomenal what's happened already," Trevor said. He added, "Lots of times it seems God shows up like in the burning bush. If you imagine that story now and say to people that God showed up in a burning bush, they would think you are crazy. A lot of doubters until the plagues showed up. I think the important thing is staying close to God. Other times it seems to me that we are in God like a fish is in the ocean, but we try to overthink and strive or contrive God into some kind of idea. I think it surpasses all understanding things and If you try to understand God, He will get close to you. I think we are allowed to go through things for not every reason we can understand. If you overthink it then you are not in life because you grab every thought and don't let life flow through you. Resistance is often suffering. I think it is about trust and faith. We don't believe a whole lot often because we can't control and our egos want to control. Then when we think like we do control we are in complete illusion. 99.9 percent of life we don't control. We can only control what we do in each moment. That's all. God can show up any way He wants. That's one of the things I love about God even though I don't understand always which version I am believing in. I love that God can use a song, a book, an overheard conversation, a triumph or tragedy to send us a message. We just don't want to be freaked out because we are all scared to death of something. Something freaks everyone out and we just don't want to be afraid. We had good times, but the fights and drinking, tidal waves over the good moments. That's why religion is such a turn-off. It feels right for me not to belong to anyone club. I guess I'm a spiritual renegade. It seems like the more attached people become to their set of beliefs the more fanatical they become in general. You might waver, but not much. To me when you talk about your faith, you make Jesus more real. You make Mary more real. Watching it on the news doesn't make me believe more or at all."

Kiana responded, "Many times I have been alone lately. I think How could you do this to me, Lord." I don't talk about this because I don't know if I will completely fall apart, but I will mention something. Mary witnessed her son be scourged and crucified. They somehow will help me in my sorrow. I have felt the Holy Spirit so strong and so much love at the same time that I was going to explode in love. The Lord is with me even in my lowest moments." Then she was silent and Trevor understood that the rest of whatever else was on Kiana's mind and heart to be left alone as her sacred suffering. He just nodded and looked back out the window at the sky. The flight was not that crowded. Subtly the slightest descent in the 737 gave notice as they made their way closer to their destination.

Chapter Twenty Nine: **Thou Shall Not**

R on packed his bags. There appeared enough circumstantial news for him to go to the gardens. He started to miss Quinn, the wilder of the two. Ron, the older and more of the conformer didn't want trouble. Quinn lived his life fast and died a slow agonizing death. Life caught up with him as he lived his life on the run as much as possible. His unofficial mantra, to bolt from life. Envy, jealousy, and greed remained the steam that seemed to be driving his life as he became older. Quinn talked to Ron and twisted inside when he saw kids go home with happy parents.

Somehow Ron seemed to be one of those people who brushed things off better than Quinn. Ron remembered that Quinn had stolen a couple of times when like gum or an album from a music store together. Ron contained a healthy fear of getting into trouble. One of the main differences, Quinn resigned to the fact that he would be getting into trouble. Ron would wince at the idea. He shared the same feelings as his brother, but with less intensity. Basic things at times became provided, but the element of unpredictability kept him on guard. His little brother looked up to him and this made him want to be the example and the steady one. His little brother, a rebel and just feistier. Ron tried to coach him and keep him out of trouble. Quinn agreed with himself that he would be in trouble anyway so why not go all out. So, he would let teachers know that his parents acted out of control. Finally, when CPS became involved again, his parents found themselves in check. However, they blamed him more than take responsibility for their own lives and the way they parented.

Quinn participated in having an affair with a married woman before he died in the hospital. What he didn't know, that Quinn excited his lover's house because her husband would show up at any moment. Quinn made his desperate getaway when he crashed into and killed Tracy. Quinn's nature, to be on the run so he always kept going. He always tried to outrun trouble. No regard for religion or God for that matter and because his parents didn't walk the walk he didn't either. With Ron in Tampa and Quinn in Austin, a phone call would be their only update from time to time. They did confide in each other because they remained best friends.

Ron warned him about the danger he put himself in and he meant at the physical, emotional and spiritual level. Quinn only paid attention though to not getting caught. He had no moral compass as surviving remained a lower-level need and he waited for another bomb to go off. His relationships at best, temporal and he never established anything long term. Whether in grade school, high school or grown-up, the pattern persisted.

Ron on the other hand somehow contained a moral compass because he sought from an early age some comfort. The only place that attractive to him, the church. He continued to look for whatever else he may need for the trip. This would be investigative in nature. Ground zero for something he looked for his whole life stood right under his nose a ninety-minute drive away. He thought about all the girls and women Quinn went through. Quinn liked being able to talk to Ron about the girls he crushed on as a kid and the women as an adult. Ron liked being his confidant. Quinn didn't feel re-spected, defended or protected so he didn't learn this. Reckless, the way he lived and the way he died. No one stood there except Ron at the end.

Ron didn't have to lie as much as Quinn who became a master at falsehood and thought he still ended up in storms anyway. Ron did have a conscience and a fear of retribution for not doing anything wrong. He existed as the designated scapegoat for his parents' poison. The fear of God and wanting to be in good graces kept Ron on track. At a young age he would remain close to God despite what he went through. Quinn, on the other hand, too fidgety and impulsive by nature to even entertain the thought. Quinn being restless did not stay in one place for long and like a wandering cowboy moved around beginning in his late teens. He surfed in the homes of friends to avoid going home himself. Quinn was edgy and because of the strain and the lack of quality time with his parents, he would not let them or anyone close to him. Deep down he craved the affection of his parents. They would either be agitated in irregular phases of ten-sion or lush over him and his brother when buzzed. Quinn's anger for his parents choosing alcohol instead of he and his brother seethed in him like an underground river. Many times he wanted to have a cookout, go out to eat or go to a movie and their plans, inebriation. At some points, his parents gave up on themselves and made a contract with dysfunction and addiction. Quinn gave up on them. Getting uprooted because of eviction or CPS became too much and all the feelings swirled around inside of him like spiritual indigestion. Quinn lived discontent and restlessness chronically and eventually sought out a way to medicate all his unattended feelings. His fears turned him into a prickly person. Being vulnerable meant he would be squashed in his unconscious mind.

Ron recalled the times when their foster parents would go to church and take him and his brother. Quinn hated going. Ron enjoyed church because for him church was like being under a waterfall. For Quinn, church was just another thing someone forced on him and that he wanted to rebel against.

Quinn got into trouble for stealing when they lived with their parents as children. When they briefly lived together in their early adulthood, Quinn would not come through on their financial arrangements thereby creating a lack of trust that amplified to the point where Ron chose to move on and did. The divide became bigger when Ron got married and then they didn't speak as they had before ever again. Quinn would come home with stuff that wasn't his and never told Ron or their parents where he got things. At home, he never got into trouble for this.

Ron worried so much about Quinn like a parent. His self-learning had taught him that in all the books he read. Ron had stepped in while his parents stepped out. He got somewhat close to their foster parents and other siblings by proxy since the foster parents had kids coming and going. A strange occurrence was to not have one's biological parents on board consistently and then having foster parents be more reliable than the biological parents. Unbeknownst to them, they had taken on their parents' egos to a degree.

Quinn did a full-on bolt after his accident with Tracy. Everyone said he killed Tracy and Quinn hearing and watching the news took him off the deep end. He became injured with a very badly broken leg and internal injuries. After the accident, he began to sink. He would have to go to a hospital sooner or later. He had killed an innocent person. Manslaughter and vehicular homicide, the words he heard on the television. He became highly sought after and he just wanted to surrender, but went instead to the hospital. The police waited for him as he drove in.

Ron never got his head around honor your father and mother. Because of their experiences, they wanted still to have a safe home environment. They had no more than an abbreviated sense of honor. They had no respect for their parents. As children, the desire to honor their parents, built into them by nature. They tried again and again. Though moments of cohesion as a family appeared rarely like a painting to be admired. Ron and Quinn didn't honor their parents because their parents lost their parental rights.

Ron would go to church at times for some spiritual spite. He and his ex-wife went on occasion but never established anything there. Keeping the Sabbath holy, not high on his list though he did try to make Sunday's a day where he rested and did nothing other than watch sports, clean his place or go out for a walk. He celebrated the Sabbath alone, by doing nothing as much as possible. Quinn never had a thought like that cross his mind. There didn't exist no rest or contemplation for Quinn. His nature, fast and he had little patience for others including himself.

Ron didn't like when Quinn took the Lord's name in vain. Quinn retorted that he would say and do whatever he pleased. He had no master, but the judge inside his head who judged him or others. Power for him, based on the fear that fueled his genuine dislike and lack of love for himself. Asking for forgiveness or humility, not his strength. Ron sensed a little relief that Quinn is gone because Quinn never seemed to be at peace with anything, at war with life. The war inside of him persisted. His passing away became the only truce.

Quinn would have no gods whereas something in Ron bought into the whole idea. Quinn's spirit pushed back and resisted everything like a baby rejecting a nursing mother. Quinn had spent much of his time dodging cars like he was trying to cross a busy interstate. He thought of Ron of just being a conformer. Ron believed in God and chose to do so without all the details of religion as he watched from the sidelines.

What shadowed Ron, the guilt he had at not being able to do more for his brother and all the bargaining the mind does going back over the stories of the past. Over and over he wondered why Quinn turned out as wild as he did. The brothers loved each other, but held different minds. He always tried to persuade Quinn and coach him up like a young football player and Quinn loved his older brother. What he never told anyone, that the only thing that settled him down, seeing Jesus on the crucifix at church.

Ron looked around his place to see if he wanted to take anything else with him. The last thing left, his bathing suit as he always liked to go in the ocean a little bit when at the beach. The gardens where he headed, located very close to the ocean. Nature spoke for itself and his spirit tuned in time after time. Expectations low. Just show up. Quietly he inquired within himself why he would go to the gardens. He looked for something to wash out his wounds. Why not?

Chapter Thirty: **I Have To Be Here**

In the past a person would never find a person like Ruth in a conversation about God. A spiritual compass in her now that pointed to the gardens. She did not share much with people about her experience. Ruth trusted Paul. Ruth was flushed spiritually and physically as she stood inconspicuously at the gardens not wanting to be noticed by people. She didn't go to see the features in the gardens. She waited on God like a child at the window, she waited in anticipation.

Ruth moseyed around the gardens as if shopper of nature. She blended in with the biggest crowd ever at the gardens. All the rumors packed the gardens like a fan-filled stadium of a team winning a lot of games. She went to the gardens to be with God. God cured her daughter of leukemia and took care of her here in the garden while she ruminated over her daughter's health and by obliterating her disbelief. Her resolve remained her steel and her loyalty ferocious for she experienced an encounter with God who took the torment away from watching her daughter being terminally ill. Her whole life led up to this moment.

She wondered what went on in Anne's mind. What does the mind of a child do with seeing the Mother of Jesus? She goes about her way and doesn't get caught up in it and make it about herself. Caught up in the right and wrong of her daughter's illness like any parent would be. Justified in her anger at God completely. Her mind became a marathon of worry with no finish line.

She exercised her mind to capacity and making every decision with worry. Her daughter only acted like she caught the flu. Ruth didn't know how to leave her mind alone because her daughter's illness became the central focus that she gave all of her effort to. She remembered what she read about Juan Diego's encounter with Mary. Anger at God and worry clogged up her spirit to the point of being a ticking time bomb. She clung to her daughter like they were boulders flying through space together.

111

"Do not fear any vexation, anxiety or pain. Do not fear any sickness or anguish. Am I not your Mother? Are you not under my mantle? Am I not your fountain of life"? Her mind and soul taken to another world and she took that world now into this world.

The afternoon sun, like the middle of summer. A hurricane moved up the eastern side of Florida, but they stood on the west coast of Florida, getting the daily dose of intense heat and humidity. The heat left one exhausted if they stayed out in the heat too long. Over 1500 people attended the gardens on this day packed like a summer jamboree. Most of all it came down to what a person believed. Some had experiences with God directly and never talked about it, some talked about their experiences and some, no personal encounters with God. The only thing for sure, Anne suffered from leukemia and now she didn't have it. The message of her healing spread and some people seemed zealous about the church who didn't believe Ruth . She didn't tell anyone that she beheld Jesus and Mary except her husband. All the kids told their parents who told everyone.

Only a few weeks passed and the general public showed up daily. The personal at the gardens just didn't know what to do. They liked the free publicity. They just didn't want free bad publicity, which is what they tried to avoid it at all costs. Mostly Catholics waited for the final authority of the Catholic Church as so many of them didn't approve by proxy. Most people didn't care about that and recognized that something was happening beyond the structure and convention of religion.

Ruth remembered her dreams and her vision. She lived in such a perpetual state of shock that she thought if she told people about what happened, her family would never live in privacy in their home again. They would have to move she thought. People at the gardens prayed so it became a prayer site within a botanical garden and most people just didn't know what to make of that. No religious statues appeared in this place, no crosses or stained glass. It seemed to be somewhat of a feeling that people showed up to a fireworks display late.

The whole experience turned Ruth into a contemplative. She didn't pray, fast or talk about peace even. A friend once shared with her something she read in a mystical text. A vision of the three Archangels approaching the mystic in a vision with heads bowed approaching above and an endless sea of clouds. At the end of the vision one of the Archangels looked up and said to the mystic, "he who is with God can do all" and then the angel bowed its head and the vision ended. At the time, a tap on the door of her soul that she dismissed as remained like a stain on her consciousness. She wasn't a shrinking violet, not about to surrender before she experienced her first encounter. After her encounter, she would never be able to read enough as her hunger and excitement about God became a powerful subtle homing device planted in her like a lighthouse.

All the courage she used to fight her daughter's leukemia did not cure her daughter's leukemia. She put everything into it. Fight or flight became a normal state as it twirled between fighting Ann's cancer and bolting from the sickness at the same time. Then she would become numb. She shut herself down as she ran out of adrenaline. Her window of tolerance closed. She told no one that in her spirit she called out and said "Jesus, I believe in you. Please help me!" This after she assailed God with blows one after the other as she wanted to put her wounds on Him. She read in the bible about Mary and her fierce love of Jesus in his passion. Going through this whole ordeal made her animal brain kick in as she would collapse and shut down. It was her body's way of surviving. In the present moment, she was focused like the tension on a crossbow.

She read about the science that occurred between our bodies and nature, the science of trauma on the brain and the science of the effect of music on the human body. Science became her deity for a form of worship. She didn't have to commit to this. A thin veil divided the difference between her belief and unbelief. Ruth didn't come from a family immersed in church and traditional religion. It remained up to her to decide on her own. Being agnostic when her daughter became ill, she became conflicted because she needed someone to be mad at.

The motivational circuits in her brain went haywire. The rage, panic, and fear created living grief in her and the separation with her daughter shortly sent her into great distress. Anne however as a child kept to being carefree to a remarkable degree and she still maintained the natural ability to play and did. Ruth kept reading to try and understand everything and stumbled across information about what went on in her own body for at least the last year. Once Anne became diagnosed with leukemia, Ruth went to hypervigilance mode and her body became like an oversized antenna for stress. Her emotional reactivity made her constantly worried and grouchy. She tried to hold off images of her daughter in a casket and hardly smiled anymore. She perseverated and looped her story to purge the trauma that lived in her. Ruth became numb. Her cognitive processing became impaired and she ran like preparing for a marathon. She reached a level of passivity and sunk into numbness before the miracle occurred. Ruth's window of tolerance for social engagement narrowed to an all-time low.

Ruth lost the ability to fall in love with life. Like a game of ping pong, her brain threw her back and forth between calm and vigilant. She was numb at every doctor's appointment that the leukemia increased in scope and her ability to be calm decreased with time. Most of the time she was frustrated like at a red light that wouldn't change.

A bright flash of lightning showed up to her right in the sky and she couldn't help, but see a storm nearing her location at the gardens as the location right next to the Florida beach. It intensified quickly as everyone looked at the sky as it happened. They stood far enough away to not feel any wind or rain, but the energy of the storm sent signals that it would be a strong one. People at the gardens didn't know whether to move or stay. They came here to see the gardens and many more came here because they heard of the things that the children said. More and more people showed up as it became later in the day as the sun made its way down the horizon. Soon the storm clouds would upon them.

The clouds closed in on them and they began to cover the sun that began its journey to twilight. The clouds built into a massive symphony as those who watched had never seen anything quite like this. Someone said "It looks like God is going to have a meeting with his angels." A preponderance of grey made up what developed into what appeared to be a tunnel leading up to the sky. Purple and violet hues laid over the grey for a sensational look and the only part of the sky where one saw the sun, the center and its brilliance, a blinding light. All around appeared lightning bolts and one looked at the spectacle that this would be something that they never saw before in this life. The higher up one looked the brighter it became. The low clouds above the ocean water became the darkest, then grey, purple, orange and bright yellow as the eye followed the tunnel up. People didn't take their eyes off of the sky. The electricity filled in the air. All the parents made sure their kids stood close to them though no one left as it became more important to them to look at the sky. It looked like the clouds of heaven encircled as they looked like mountains going up to the sky. Like an expansive landscape of mountain scenery that went off as far as the eye, the clouds did the same thing going upward. The center now of the tower went straight up to a blinding light at the top. It became a symphony of nature. It looked so grand it made everyone small as the power of nature blew up. The lightning bolts in the sky kept everyone on edge. Those who came today for spiritual reasons believed that something remarkable would take place. They looked up into heaven. Nobody moved and everything became still. A silence in the air, the quietest thing. The calm, evident, like all of creation waited.

The hair on the backs of everyone's head began to stand up as the air became electrified. Everyone remained still. Something started to happen, The little kids looked up at the sky at the majestic landscape that seemed to come from nowhere. Everyone started to experience an enormous amount of love.

Chapter Thirty One: **Children!**

T he weather theater in front of the crowd looked as dramatic and pic-turesque as ever. The sky, however, became progressively illuminated. All of the people at the garden including Kiana, Trevor, Ron, Ruth and ev-eryone else, captured and seeing all of the sudden the azures of heaven in radiant splendor. The whole scene flooded with the light of paradise as a blessedness overcame everyone in the crowd. The expanse of the heavenly kingdom appeared above everything before them. Then came forth heaven. It looked like an entirely different world opened up upon every soul. Even though it looked far away, the view appeared as distinct as anything. At the same time, everyone sensed that heaven looked so far away and yet they were transported distinctly to that place. They had all been taken away from the earth and taken far away. The look of paradise seemed to go on forever. No one was aware of anything that went on around them except what the eyes of their kneeling souls saw.

At that very instant began to appear what looked like fireflies in a twilights' meadow. Meandering about and flickering in different locations. Then everyone beheld the flickering flames. All present, stunned and now began to appear a lady whose appearance looked equally beautiful and gentle. A blue mist had appeared and from it, she emerged with her hands clasped over her chest. Her dress, blue on the outside and a shim-mering white on the outside. A brilliant light pervaded her being as the mantle overhead flowed down over her like a gown of divinity. A holy white light illuminated her and the appearance of her face appeared as sweet and gentle as anyone might imagine it to be. Her face looked inviting with her gaze looking down and the whole crowd mystified. She began to open her arms and the palms of her hands radiating a light that seemed to travel from her heart and hands in all directions. She appeared beautiful beyond description. Her gown, made of light. She looked up now at all those before her. Golden light enveloped everyone as everyone witnessed the boundless blue skies of God. The Holy Spirit above her head with His wings wide open. They all appeared in a cone and cloak of light. Ruth, the only one who managed a question, "who are you"? Looking into the souls of all before her, "I am the Mother of the Truth who became flesh in me. Children of the earth, I come here today to tell you I do not reproach. I just love! I do not condemn. You do not love one another. You do not feel yourselves to be brothers and sisters. Come that I may take you to Christ while holding your hand in mine. Whoever loves me loves the Son of my flesh. I will lead you to the light of God.

I am the Mystical Rose and am full of grace. I embraced pain and love together. How many of you trample on God to be gods. The road from Bethlehem to Egypt was marked by my tears. My Son in the temple became an initial appeal to hearts that God's hour was at hand. I am the Mother under the cross, but the supernatural sorrow is the hatred oppressing my Son. A boundless sea of hatred growing in the world. I as your Mother suffer so much from seeing you my children cut off from the firstborn and brother in heaven who is Jesus. When I received my Son from the cross, my womb became lacerated.

I am the new Eve. Take your sorrows with me to God. Do not be afraid. God provides divine aid. Let all that is not your Master fall away. Be alive and concern yourself with Jesus as Life. Follow My Son and neglect everything that is not His voice. Every heart is a small kingdom of God on the earth. The earth is now a forest of idols and every heart is an altar, but seldom ever occupied by God. It is sorrowful and bitter to abandon the Lord. Come to serve Jesus and it only takes an act of goodwill. Every good deed is the origin of great things, which you do not imagine. In everything turn your eyes to God. One of the errors made by man is to possess a lack of honesty towards himself.

Science is vanity and increasing human knowledge while increasing the affliction of the spirit. It is vanity because you are not bridled with supernatural wisdom and the holy love of God. Jesus is everywhere. He knows everything and can do everything. He is God. The hours of temptation come and can diminish souls with disappointments and disagreements. If your soul brims with faith, you can overcome it. How can man answer his questions if God is not with him to give him the answers?

Love is affection from soul to soul so that man does not view his companion as a slave. Whatever is not love is vice. My Son only speaks of love and whatever is not love is not the truth. Loving God and loving your neighbor is

117

the way that truth is found. Who can disclose the mysteries of creation, but our Creator? My Son is here for you to lead you back to grace.

My son teaches you kindly and patiently. In truth, honesty and in moral behavior are neither adjustments nor compromises. God is eternal and with no beginning or end. Do not reject God even in the smallest things. Those of you my children who accept my son's doctrine will not bring pain in one's ego, but liberation. I urge you before it is too late. Do you wish to be fatigued, desolate and tired, when you can be relieved and consoled? You are now desolate. You grieve my Jesus with your pride. Be humble and accept the reproach of God and promise that you want perfection for divine purposes. Come to my Jesus. He corrects and understands you. You are suffering material, moral and spiritual sorrows. Blessed are those who follow my Son and trust Him even in the darkness. Persevere on your journey to God and remove all relish for human things. I urge you, children! Come to my Son those who are tired and fatigued because of the loneliness and sorrow of the world. The spirit of my son is not heavy. Embrace his doctrine as a bride. My Son will give you rest for your souls. Meekness and humility will triumph among whom you conquer with love. My Son wants you with Him in His Kingdom. Strive to be like Him. The yoke of Jesus is sweet and its weight is light. The glory that you will have if you are faithful to Him is infinitely powerful and eternal."

Suddenly, all of the flickering flames that hovered above the ground turned into angels and they encircled The Blessed Mother. Mary, after addressing all the people. changed her gaze from them to looking upward to heaven while all the angels had their heads down in reverence. Suddenly, the whole entourage began to rise upwards towards the sky. They slowly disappeared up into the blue mist from whence they came. The sky then lit up with lightning and thunder that continued for a long time to allow all of those present to come back to where they stood before. The gardens had gone back to prior state. Each person exploded with love as the Holy Spirit made a final pass through the crowd.

Chapter Thirty Two: **Who Is This Man?**

An overwhelming peace, stillness, and love overwhelmed each person that day. Eli wanted his children to be close to him and to not be afraid of their father like many children are. He wanted to banish any fears that his people had of him. Eli loved all people in his life and those who would be in the future. To love and to be love others was important to him. He had so much hope for people and nations. With was so much tumult in the world now, so many people lost touch with the most essential part of them.

Eli thought about all of the people and how many of them have lost hope in life. If the world was more familiar with God, they would have much more peace and security within themselves. He loved it when he ran into people in the gardens and everywhere. He was just starting his next walk on the beach. Wherever he was he peered into the faces of those around him and was able to be in their hearts with an uncanny ability. He kept to his creating as much beauty in nature as possible especially working at the gardens his whole life. He was always coming to people just as he is and he was concerned for everybody it seemed as paternity was natural for him.

Eli was making himself available for people and he wanted them to be able to trust like they once did a long time ago. When he worked in the garden, he watched over all the people there as they came and went, for he had worked there longer than anyone. All the people were his children in his own eyes. He enjoyed contemplating all the work he had done there for he looked at the gardens like his masterpiece and even more so the people who visited there. He got close to people thereby watching them and he loved how they got to see the gardens and work he had done without trying to take any credit for it ever. His greatest happiness was in being with the people and talking with them like a father and his children.

Eli's body was aging. Eternity did not escape him. Those who described him said that he had this youthful eternal look about him, but always loving nonetheless. The gardens were at first a thought in his mind and then he spoke his dream into being. He used all of his power to create gardens for people. He loved people and his greatest happiness was in loving them and being with them. He had to create the gardens before the people would come. He had built it in his mind before it became a reality. He loved how people would stroll, investigate and share their experiences of the garden with one another even in silence. All the materials had to come first as plants and trees were the foundation for the garden that would provide sustenance for a system that would be a tapestry of life to be enjoyed and shared. Slowly he created the garden from scratch one living thing at a time and used the air, sun, and rain so that everything would grow. His infinite generosity showed itself as people of all sorts came to the gardens. He desired to show them joy when they came to the gardens. He loved the peaceful people and those who were clothed in vices.

He saw how people created disorder in their lives. His son had always been part of the plan and came to the gardens at the right time for things to be right. Many storms brought destruction to the gardens and the flood from many years ago all but ruined everything. Everyone said his son was just like him who was loving, pure of heart and merciful.

By observing the people who came to the garden over the years he was able to have his finger on the disorder and ingratitude that people generally had toward life. The world experienced calamities because of spiritual neglect and he noticed that people's faith was often corrected after the destruction of possessions or war. Eli was proud of his son and what he represented. Eli, a father, a brother and a close friend as he sometimes struck up relationships among those whom one might say he was just. Nature was God's expression of love that he wished to share with them. It was for enjoyment and healing. Rather they took advantage of it by not valuing it.

Eli saw that the general population in the U.S. had gotten away from God. The atmosphere had become one of the indulgences in technology and materialism while they neglected spirit, nature, and divinity. He thought that if the world were to follow the ten commandments that they would save themselves so much suffering by making God their first love and by seeking first the kingdom of God inside themselves. Because man had forgotten God, they had sunk into error and fear. People have made up laws according to their whims, which seemed easier for them to follow. Somehow because of people's fear of God that was exaggerated, they began to slink away from the source of their being.

God had visited men through prophets and still it wasn't enough to keep man close to God. Even God himself living among men was not enough to the point that they killed him. Eli loved people and even after the garden was near destruction, he never waned in his love for people. He had taken so many steps to restore the garden to the way it once was. Eli had a lighthearted way of looking at people. By loving God and each other, man's indifference would expatiate. By excluding God, man was separating himself from God and all the graces available to them. Through his son, people enjoyed all the benefits of creation that were available to them. He thought that if people honored God that they would not live in idolatry, paganism, false and evil sects that lead to eternal suffering. The world clung to its materialism and advances in technology in vain. These things were distracting people from God.

God lives close to the man and follows him everywhere. He supplies everything. Eli was aware of all the toils and desires and that people were afraid that they were going to be cast into a terrifying hell. Eli loved his children more than a mother loves her child and loved his children even when they left their families. The world would be a much better place if families honored God in their homes and depended on him for all their needs. People didn't realize that God is reaching out to them ceaselessly. God was close to people in the things that happened to them and around them. He wanted to take care of the whole world who as a whole succumbed more and more to the vices which, little by little were leading them to ruin.

Walking along the beach Eli encountered a young man digging in the sand and offered "Are you looking for something? You look very busy." "Did you hear what happened yesterday. I mean everyone around here is talking about it. The Virgin Mary appeared and everyone is beside themselves with this enormous revelation or apparition. We came here because Mary was appearing to little children and then the lady who had a daughter who was cured of leukemia and herself was an atheist," Trevor said in wonderment as he looked at Eli.

Eli responded, "it was God reaching out as a friend and as a confidant. Sometimes people will be an eyewitness to God's love. The Holy Spirit is the interplay of the Creator or the Father and the Son. Jesus is in the Father and the Father is in him. The ocean next to us and as far as you can see is water. In the same way, God is an ocean of mercy and charity. God is preparing great glory for people in eternity. He loves all people regardless of age, country, status, societies, sects, believers, unbelievers and the indifferent. All creatures of humanity are enfolded in this love.

Dive into the ocean of God's charity so that any who are bitter by faults and sins may be bathed with love. Cast yourself into this ocean and remain in it forever. Now is the time of many graces from God. God is personal and tender meeting all your needs.

Trevor responded, "you know a lot about God. I have been trying to figure this whole thing out and then this apparition happens. I've been searching for different belief systems to learn about it all because they each have their own story. I think God is so deep, broad, wide and complicated that we will never figure it all out because we are not made with the capacity to understand everything even though its already been figured out."

Eli answered back that "God is worthy of praise and love forever. To love and honor God is the first commandment. Jesus is to be honored and respected for all the insults that were hurled upon him by Pontius Pilate and others. He was insulted and his holy and innocent humanity was scourged. God wants everyone to know their King. The Father wants people honoring his son. He wants people to be just."

Trevor couldn't believe he was having this deep conversation about God with a stranger who just walked up on the beach, but he liked it and it was as if this man understood all his longing and searches for a truth that permeates all truths. He kept on, "people have all these different faiths, but how do we figure which one is real? It seems like people are born into traditions and then they get to make up their mind whether they want to stay with it or not."

Eli came back with "there are many superstitions in the world and many people acknowledge God, but they do not see that God wants to be close to them and that He is their maker. There are many distractions in the world now with technology, materialism and busy everyday life. God understands people have sorrows and dejection. More people would convert and be close to God if they knew how much he cared for them. People no matter where in the world do not know God as He is because, amid all their ideas about God, they don't understand that God is the most tender of fathers and that God wants to transform their love, which is blocked by all their fears of God."

Trevor asked, "how can anyone relate to God who is so big and powerful? No one can put their minds around it and then we end up having all these ideas about God and defending them against other ideas. It just creates a lot of turmoil in the world."

"People do not comprehend God as he is so God made himself similar to creatures so they would begin to understand. Because they only think of God as terrifyingly just without realizing that God wants to help to make their earthly lives easier. People who call upon God will not perish." Eli went on to say, that "God wants to melt the ice of evil that suffocates souls. People who work for God's glory and who commit themselves to God will be blessed because God does count everything, even the smallest effort people make. Until society acknowledges God and worships him, they will fall to the laws of the devil, slavery and live in tyranny. God as a father sees everything, knows everything and provides everything. God forgives easily and only punishes reluctantly. If people turn to God their burdens will be lightened and their hard lives sweetened."

Trevor went on to say "people seem to live in darkness in the world. Even though I didn't live in prior generations in the last century, it seems like life looked much simpler and slower before technology and the internet took over. Technology is awesome and we can learn anything in a snap, but people are not close, they don't seem to be strong or salt of the earth. People seem to be more insecure and isolated and they live virtual lives as much as a real ones because of the modern era. Most people's minds are not on God."

And Eli answered, "God is like a sun that warms and his life is a permanent reality and his love is passionate. You talk about this century being privileged more than others and that is true. A divine touch is missing from the world. Time is pressing on and God doesn't want anyone to be afraid of anything though fear is growing much in the world. God wants to help people in their efforts and wants souls to be joyful and peaceful. Mary came to urge the world to share a devotion to the sacred heart of her son and for people to recognize God the Father through his son. What God also wants is man's confidence, his love, and his gratitude. Yesterday God stooped down to share his glory with people and used his daughter as a messenger of that glory and to shake the world of its spiritual slumber. Great numbers of people are falling into unhappiness with the evil in the world. This is not the purpose of creation. God is waiting for his prodigal people to return to him with fervor. The world is being divided by doubt and disbelief with all its sacrilegious people, heretics and all the like. Their ignorance is now being addressed by things like the apparition of yesterday."

Trevor couldn't believe all the things this man said. He looked very old around 80 though somehow, he revealed this youthful magnetizing gentle smile. His blue eyes, comforting. He just walked up from nowhere. Trevor tried to figure it all out. "With so many paths to God, how can everyone be on the same page, ever?" he asked.

God loves people to be apostles of his work. This, in turn, makes people strong and powerful. Then people are inspired and God puts them in the right frame of mind. This is how men will be conquered and saved. God wants people to enjoy great confidence in him and to just behave as his children. People don't need to mortify themselves and live in austerity. People don't need to be barefoot and cover themselves in ashes, but just to trust in God. God can do all and make himself small so he can make you great. Unbelievers live in impious communities and think that God is asking the impossible of them and that God wants them to be a slave, to be distant from his subjects and make them respectful and devout. He does require that the commandments are observed and that man be not like animals and hide evil inclinations. God gave each person a treasure and that is their soul. God wants to be loved with a special devotion to give benefits to people and let them share in his power, a glory so that man can be happy. God wants to love you and be loved by you. Respect for God out of fear keeps man distant from God. This is false respect and a wound to the heart of God. So much ill respect of God that leads men to idolatry and division. Don't be led by the enemy, but by the truth. The evil one cheats you by making you afraid of God.

Trevor looked at Eli like the loving father that he needed most of his life. His parents lived caught up on their wounds that they never seem to overcome. Talking to Eli felt like talking to the father or grandfather whose every word you hung onto. He said to Eli, "Some people only understand the religion they grew up in. What then is the true way with so many ways?"

Eli answered, "True religion is recognizing He who created you and wants you to be saved. God is about truth and salvation. People think that God creates them and leaves them alone. God is following people everywhere and protecting people and is very liberal towards people who forget his goodness.

"The one thing or appeal of Christianity over the others is the person-hood of Jesus. Jesus is God becoming a person so we can get our head around it all and relate" Trevor said.

Eli understands what Trevor said and told him, "it pleases God when people honor him and don't overburden themselves. God wants to serve with simplicity. God is both King and Friend. Look at the crucifix and realize the extent to which God loves them. You cannot taste freedom if you do not live in the truth. Deep in their hearts, people suffer because they do not experience true peace or joy because they do not enjoy the one who created them. People who do not follow the true law are led by vice into evil. These people are not happy and their hearts are not at ease. Can a human heart be at ease by finding joy only in human pleasures? No one will be truly happy unless one does submit to God as their creator."

How come then does God show up as the God of the old testament in severity. People who read those things would be afraid of God. I think that's the kind of thing that makes people afraid of God. Why does he do that?" Trevor inquired.

"God punished those in the old testament because they began to act like animals and they were reminded that they are not animals. Jesus came as the perfect Son through God who adopted people and since then people are called children and not creatures. Man is reminded that he is distinguishable from animals and without trusting God as their father, no one is truly free."

"Sounds like you are saying that if people trust God and honor him, God will give them peace and relief from worries, troubles, and sufferings" Trevor added. "Yes", Eli said "and if people honor their father, businesses, and families honor God, God will give them peace. The spirit of peace will come down upon them. If the different countries in the world did this, there would be no more war because there will be no war where God is. If people called upon God, they will win victory over their enemy. God is perfect holiness and he wants his children to be as such. Through the Holy Spirit and his son God offers his holiness. God comes to people through the Holy Spirit. God is waiting for people to ask him for the holiness and perfection they need and nothing will be refused wherein God enjoys his repose. The favorite place to be for God is in a human heart. This is the most beautiful tabernacle."

Trevor took it all in and looked down and away from Eli's gaze. He went on, "the world is chaotic because it leaves God out of the picture. So many distractions, it is easy to take your mind off of God. Especially with technology and the sophisticated acquisition of knowledge. The world is superficial and I thought we would be moving forward, but we are moved backward. Everybody gets offended over everything and you can't say what you want anymore. So, it seems less free like that. The country doesn't seem to be as whole as it used to be and people are much more to themselves. We've forgotten our roots somehow. The world feels less secure. What you're saying is that if people would turn to God, more order would exist in the world with a lot more peace among people and in themselves." Trevor stuck out his hand and introduced himself. "I'm Trevor. Been nice talking to you, sir."

"I'm Eli. Been nice talking to you as well son. Enjoy the rest of this beautiful day. So now you understand that a world without God is insane" he said in a deep and serene tone as he turned to walk away.